Goblin Tales of Lancashire

by James Bowker

Originally published 1878

Flying High Press

Cover Artwork: James Joel

ISBN-13: 978-1977524676

CONTENTS

INTRODUCTION.

For many of the superstitions which still cling to him the Lancashire man of the present day is indebted to his Celtic and Scandinavian ancestors. From them the Horse and Worm stories, and the Giant lore of the northern and southern mountains and fells, have come down, while the relationship of the 'Jinny Greenteeth,' the presiding nymph of the ponds and streams, with allusions to whom the Lancastrian mother strives to deter her little ones from venturing near the pits and brooks; to the water-spirits of the Gothic mythology, is too evident to admit of any doubt. The source of the 'Gabriel Ratchets,' the hell-hounds whose fear-inspiring yelps still are heard by the benighted peasant, who finds in the dread sound a warning of the approach of the angel of death; in the Norse Aasgaardsveia, the souls condemned to ride about the world until doomsday, and who gallop through the midnight storm with shrieks and cries which ring over the lonely moors; or in that other troop of souls of the brave ones who had died in battle, being led by the storm-god Woden to Walhalla, also is undeniable.

Striking, however, as are the points of similitude between some of the Lancastrian traditions and those of the north of Europe, others seem to be peculiar to the county, and that these are of a darker and gloomier cast than are the superstitions of districts less wild and mountainous, and away from the weird influence of the sea, with its winter thunderings suggestive of hidden and awful power, may in a great measure be correctly attributed to the nature of the scenery.

It is easy to understand how the unlettered peasant would people with beings of another world either the bleak fells, the deep and gloomy gorges, the wild cloughs, the desolate moorland wastes two or three thousand feet above the level of the sea, of the eastern portion of the county; or the salt marshes where the breeze-bent and mysterious-looking trees waved their spectral boughs in the wind; the dark pools fringed with reeds, amid which the 'Peg-o'-Lantron' flickered and danced, and over which came the hollow cry of the bittern and the child-like plaint of the plover; and the dreary glens, dark lakes, and long stretches of sand of the north and west.

To him the forest, with its solemn Rembrandtesque gloom, where Druids erst heard victims groan,

the lonely fir-crowned pikes, and the mist-shrouded mountains, would seem fitting homes for the dread shapes whose spite ended itself in the misfortunes and misery of humanity. Pregnant with mystery to such a mind would be the huge fells, with their shifting 'neetcaps' of cloud, the towering bluffs, the swampy moors, and trackless morasses, across which the setting sun cast floods of blood-red light; and irresistible would be the influence of such scenery upon the lonely labourer who would go about his daily tasks with a feeling that he was surrounded by the supernatural.

And wild as are many parts of the county to-day, it is difficult to conceive its condition a century or two ago, when much of the land was not only uncultivated, but was, for at least a portion of the year, covered by sheets of water, the highways being little more than bridle roads, or, if wider than usual, very sloughs of despond, the carts in several of the rural districts being laid aside in winter as utterly useless, and grain and other commodities, even in summer time, being conveyed from place to place on the backs of long strings of pack-horses.

Living in lonely houses and cottages shut out from civilisation by the difficulties of communication, and hemmed in by floating mists and by much that was awe-inspiring, with in winter additional barriers of storm, snow and flood, it is easy to imagine how in the fancy of the yeoman, shepherd, farmer, or solitary lime burner, as 'th' edge o' dark' threw its weird glamour over the scene, boggarts and phantoms would begin to creep about to the music of the unearthly voices heard in every sough and sigh of the wandering wind as it wailed around the isolated dwellings.

In everything weird they found a message from the unknown realms of death. The noise of the swollen waters of the Ribble or the Lune, or the many smaller streams hurrying down to the sea, was to them the voice of the Water Spirit calling for its victim, and the howling of their dogs bade the sick prepare to meet 'the shadow with the keys.' All around them were invisible beings harmful or mischievous, and to them they traced much of the misfortune which followed the stern working of nature's laws.

The superstitions which date from, as well as the actual annals of the Witch Mania in Lancashire, in some slight degree confirm this theory, for whereas in the flat and more thickly-populated districts the hag contented herself with stealing milk from her neighbour's cows, spoiling their bakings, and other practical jokes of a comparatively harmless kind, in the wilder localities--the region of pathless moors and mist-encircled mountains--the witch ever was raising terrible storms, bringing down the thunder, killing the cattle, dealing out plagues and pestilence at will, wreaking evil of every conceivable kind upon man and beast, and, hot from her sabbath of devil-worship, even casting the sombre shadows and dread darkness of death over the households of those who had fallen under the ban of her hate.

Lancashire has, however, an extensive ghost lore to which this theory has no reference, consisting as it does of stories of haunted houses and churchyards, indelible blood-stains, and all the paraphernalia of theShapes that walkAt dead of night, and clank their chains and waveThe torch of hell around the murderer's bed.

The sketch in this volume, 'Mother and Child,' for the skeleton of which tradition I am indebted to the late Mr. J. Stanyan Bigg, may be considered a fair specimen of these stories. In most cases these legends are not simply the vain creations of ignorance and darkness, although they fade before the light of knowledge like mists before the sun, for under many of them may be found a moral and a warning, or a testimony to the beauty of goodness, hidden it is true beneath the covering of a rude fable, just as inscriptions rest concealed below the moss of graveyards. The well-known legend of the Boggart of Townley Hall, with its warning cry of 'Lay out, lay out!' and its demand for a victim every seventh year, is a striking example of traditions of this class--emphatic protests against wrong, uttered in the form of a nerve-affecting fable. In more than one of the stories of this kind to which I have listened, the ghost of the victim has re-visited 'the pale glimpses of the moon,' and made night so hideous to the wrong-doer, that, in despair and remorse, he has put an end to himself; and trivial as these things may seem to Mr. Gradgrind and his school, they have, like other and nobler parables, influenced minds impervious to dry fact.

To the devil lore of the county, however, the theory certainly will apply, for surely it is in a gloomy gorge, through which forked lightnings flash and chase each other, and the thunder rolls and reverberates, or on a dark and lonesome moor, rather than upon the shady side of Pall Mall, one would expect to meet the Evil One.

Yet, undoubtedly, other causes contributed to enrich the store of tales of fiends with which the county abounds.

In Lancashire many of the old customs, even such as the riding of the wooden Christ on Palm Sunday, continued to be kept up at a later period than was the case in other parts of England; and, notwithstanding the prohibitory edicts of the commissioners appointed by Queen Elizabeth, Miracle Plays and Moralities doubtless were performed there even during the early part of the reign of James I., for the Reformation, rapidly as its principles took root and spread in other parts of the country, did not make rapid headway in Lancashire, where great numbers of the people remained true to the faith of their forefathers. In fact, in many parishes, long after the Church of England had been by law established, Catholic priests continued to be the only officiating ministers. Probably the people loved their church not only on account of its doctrines, of which it may be presumed most of them knew but little, and of its impressive ceremonies, but also because of its recognition of the holy days and fair days, wakes, and games it was powerless to suppress; and perhaps of all the amusements thus winked at or even patronised by the church, that of dramatic representations, rude and grotesque as they undoubtedly were, was the most important. In many places the members of the various guilds and brotherhoods were the performers, but in the majority of cases the entertainments were given by the priests and other ecclesiastical functionaries.

What part the Devil played in these amusements is well known to the antiquary, the old accounts containing particulars of the expenditure upon not only hair for the Evil One's wig, but also for canvas, of which to construct black shirts for the Satanic tag-rag, or, as the old scribes plainly put it, 'for the damned.' It is evident from the old records that Satan left the hands of his dresser an object compared with which the most hideous jack-in-the-box of the modern toy shop would be a vision of loveliness; and, as his chief occupations were those of roaring and yelling, and of suffering all sorts of indignities at the hands of the Vice, as does the pantaloon at the hands of the clown in a pantomime of to-day, it is easy to see that his _rôle_ was not a very dignified one. Everywhere the stage devil was simply the stage fool. Even in France, where the drama ever has been submitted to precise rules, 'there was,' as Albert Reville has remarked (_Histoire du Diable, ses origines, sa grandeur et sa decadence._ Strasbourg: 1870), 'a class of popular pieces called devilries (_diableries_), gross and often obscene masquerades, in which at least four devils took part.... In Germany also the devil was diverting on the stage. There exists an old Saxon Mystery of the Passion, in which Satan repeats, like a mocking echo, the last words of Judas who hangs himself; and when, in accordance with the sacred tradition, the traitor's bowels fall asunder, the Evil One gathers them into a basket, and, as he carries them away, sings a little melody appropriate to the occasion.' Undoubtedly these misrepresentations of the apostate angel helped to familiarise the popular mind with the idea of a personal devil going about veritably seeking whom he might devour; and although, when with the crowd in the presence of the Thespian ecclesiastics, people might feel quite at home with, and really enjoy, the company of the Evil One, away again on the dreary moor, or in the lonely hillside cottage, with the night wind howling at the door, fear would resume its wonted supremacy, and the feeling would be deepened and intensified by the memory of the horrid appearance of the stage Satan.

It is possible that in a great measure we owe to these performances the somewhat monotonous frequency with which, in the purely local Lancashire devil stories, the Evil One, who generally in the most stupid manner permits himself to be overreached, comes oft second best, for doubtless many of the traditions were moulded in accordance with the lot of Satan in the miracle plays, as, in their turn, these were, although perhaps indirectly, based upon the teachings of the church, and that, in its turn, upon the writings of the Fathers, some of whom, and notably Origen, did not hesitate to speak of the Redemption even as due in no small degree to Satanic stupidity, a view so lastingly predominant in the Church that as Reville has said, 'la poesie ecclésiastique, la prédication populaire, des enseignements pontificaux même le repandirent, le dramatisèrent, le consacrèrent partout.'

An interesting chapter in the history of religious beliefs might be written upon the views of the early Fathers with reference to Satan and his legion, and the student is not inclined to be quite so severe upon the superstitions of the unlettered peasant when he finds Jerome recording it as the opinion of all the doctors in the church, that the air between heaven and earth is filled with Evil Spirits, and Augustine and others stating that the devils had fallen there from a higher and purer region of the air. The early Christian Church too had its order of _Exorcists_, who had care of those possessed by Evil Spirits, the _energumeni_, and the Bishops, departing from the original idea that laymen had the power of exorcism, ordained men to the office and called upon them to exercise their functions even before the rite of baptism, to deliver the candidates 'from the dominion of the power of darkness.'

Of the lighter superstitions in Lancashire, that of belief in fairies appears to be almost extinct, and it is to be lamented that forty years ago folk lore was considered of so little importance, for the slight and vague references in a rare little 'History of Blackpool,' by the Rev. W. Thornber, upon two of which the sketches entitled 'The Silver Token,' and 'The Fairy's Spade' are founded, show that the task of gathering a goodly store of such vestiges of ancient faiths would at the time when that volume was written have been a comparatively easy one. To-day, however, the case is different. Even my friend, the late Mr. John Higson, of Lees, to whose kindness I owe the tradition upon which the story of 'The King of the Fairies' is based, and whose labours in out-of-the-way paths dear to antiquaries were for some years as untiring as successful and praiseworthy, was not able to gather much bearing upon the fairy mythology of the Lancashire people.

Most of the fairy and folk stories it was my good fortune to hear in the county and moorland districts were of a conventional kind, lubber fiends, death warnings, fairy ointment, and fairy money being as plentiful as diamonds in Eastern tales, and for that reason it was not thought necessary to reproduce them in this volume.

The darker forms of superstition, like lower organisms, are more tenacious of life, and in many a retired nook of Lancashire there still may be found small congregations of believers in all the mystic lore of devildom and witchcraft. Readers of Mr. Edwin Waugh's exquisite sketches of north country life will at once call to mind, in the 'Grave of the Griselhurst Boggart,' an illustration of that dim fear of the supernatural which is yet so all-powerful, while the valuable collection of Folk Lore from the pens of the late Mr. Wilkinson and Mr. John Harland is full of testimony to the vitality of many of these offshoots from old-world creeds.

GOBLIN TALES OF LANCASHIRE.

TH' SKRIKER (SHRIEKER).

On a fine night, about the middle of December, many years ago, a sturdy-looking young fellow left Chipping for his cottage, three or four miles away, upon the banks of the Hodder. The ground was covered with snow, which in many places had drifted into heaps, and the keen frost had made the road so slippery that the progress he made was but slow. Nature looked very beautiful, and the heart of the rustic even was touched by the sweet peacefulness of the scene. The noble old Parlick, and the sweeping Longridge, with its fir-crowned Thornley Height and Kemple End, stood out boldly against the clear sky, and the moon shed her soft silvery light into the long silent valley, stretching away until its virgin paleness mingled with the shadows and the darkness of the distant fells beyond Whitewell.

All was still, save when the sighing wind rustled gently through the frosted branches of the leafless trees by the roadside, and shook down upon the wayfarer a miniature shower of snow; for even the tiny stream, so full of mirth and music in the summer time, had been lulled to sleep by the genius of winter; and the cottagers, whose little houses, half-hidden by the rime, seemed hardly large enough for the dwellings of dwarfs, had been snugly sleeping for hours.
Adam was by no means a timid or nervous being, but there was a nameless something in the deathly silence which oppressed, if it did not actually frighten, him; and although he sang aloud a verse of the last song he had heard before he left the kitchen of the Patten Arms, his voice had lost its heartiness. He earnestly wished himself safely across the little bridge over the brook; but he was yet some distance from the stream when the faint chimes of midnight fell upon the air. Almost immediately after the last stroke of twelve had broken the silence a cloud passed over the face of the moon, and comparative darkness enveloped the scene; the wind, which before had been gentle and almost noiseless, began to howl amid the boughs and branches of the waving trees, and the frozen snow from the hedgerows was dashed against the wayfarer's face.

He had already begun to fancy that he could distinguish in the soughing of the wind and the creaking of the boughs unearthly cries and fiendish shouts of glee; but as he approached the dreaded stream his courage almost entirely failed him, and it required a great effort to keep from turning his back to it, and running away in the direction of the little village at the foot of Parlick. It struck him, however, that he had come a long distance; that if he did go back to the Patten Arms the company would be dispersed, and the inmates asleep, and, what was more effective than all, that if he could only cross the bridge he would be safe, the Greenies, Boggarts, and Feorin not having power over any one who had passed over the water. Influenced by this thought, yet with his knees trembling under him, he pushed forward with assumed boldness, and he had almost reached the bridge when he heard the noise of passing feet in the crunching snow, and became conscious of the presence of a ghastly thing he was unable to see. Suddenly a sepulchral howl brought him to a stop, and, with his heart throbbing loudly enough to be heard, he stood gazing fixedly into the darkness. There was nothing to be perceived, however, save the copings of the bridge, with their coverings of rime; and he might have stood there until daylight had not another cry, louder and even more unearthly and horrible than the preceding one, called him from his trance. No sooner had this second scream died away than, impelled by an irresistible impulse, he stepped forward in the direction whence the noise had come. At this moment the moon burst forth from behind the clouds which had for some time obscured her light, and her rays fell upon the road, with its half-hidden cart-tracks winding away into the dim distance; and in the very centre of the bridge he beheld a hideous figure with black shaggy hide, and huge eyes closely resembling orbs of fire.

Adam at once knew from the likeness the dread object bore to the figure he had heard described by those who had seen the Skriker, that the terrible thing before him was an Ambassador of Death.

Without any consciousness of what he was doing, and acting as though under the sway of a strange and irresistible mesmeric influence, he stepped towards the bridge; but no sooner did he stir than the frightful thing in front of him, with a motion that was not walking, but rather a sort of heavy gliding, moved also, slowly retreating, pausing when he paused, and always keeping its fiery eyes fixed upon his blanched face. Slowly he crossed the stream, but gradually his steps grew more and more rapid, until he broke into a run. Suddenly a faint knowledge of the horrible nature of his position dawned upon him. A little cottage stood by the roadside, and from one of its chamber-windows, so near to the ground as to be within his reach, a dim light shone, the room probably being occupied by a sick person, or by watchers of the dead. Influenced by a sudden feeling of companionship, Adam tried to cry out, but his tongue clave to his parched mouth, and ere he could mumble a few inarticulate sounds, scarcely audible to himself, the dwelling was left far behind, and a sensation of utter loneliness and helplessness again took possession of him.

He had thus traversed more than a mile of the road, in some parts of which, shaded by the high hedgerows and overhanging boughs, the only light seemed to him to be that from the terrible eyes, when suddenly he stumbled over a stone and fell. In a second, impressed by a fear that the ghastly object would seize him, he regained his feet, and, to his intense relief, the Skriker was no longer visible. With a sigh of pleasure he sat down upon a heap of broken stones, for his limbs, no longer forced into mechanical movement by the influence of the spectre's presence, refused to bear him further. Bitterly cold as was the night, the perspiration stood in beads upon his whitened face, and, with the recollection of the Skriker's terrible eyes and horrible body strong upon him, he shook and shivered, as though in a fit of the ague. A strong and burly man, in the very prime of life, he felt as weak as a girl, and, fearing that he was about to sink to the ground in a swoon, he took handfuls of the crisp snow and rubbed them upon his forehead. Under this sharp treatment he soon revived a little, and, after several unsuccessful efforts, he succeeded in regaining his feet, and resumed his lonely journey.

Starting at the least sough of the breeze, the faintest creak of a bending branch, or the fall of a piece of frozen rime from a bough, he slowly trudged along.

He had passed the quaint old house at Chaigely, the sudden yelp of a chained dog in the court-yard giving him a thrill of horror as he went by, and he had reached the bend in that part of the road which is opposite the towering wood-covered Kemple End. A keen and cutting blast swept through the black firs that crowned the summit, and stood, like solemn sentinels, upon the declivity. There was a music in the wind mournful as a croon over the corpse of a beautiful woman, whose hair still shimmers with the golden light of life; but Adam heard no melody in the moaning sighs which seemed to fill the air around. To him, whose soul was yet under the influence of the terror through which he had so recently passed, the sounds assumed an awful nature; whilst the firs, standing so clearly defined against the snow, which lay in virgin heaps upon the beds of withered fern, seemed like so many weird skeletons shaking their bony arms in menace or in warning.

With a suddenness that was more than startling, there was a lull, and the breeze ceased even to whisper. The silence was more painful than were the noises of the blast battling with the branches, for it filled the breast of the solitary wayfarer with forebodings of coming woe. At the point he had reached the road sank, and as Adam stepped into the almost utter darkness, caused by the high banks, to which clung masses of decayed vegetation, beautified by the genius of winter into white festoons, again and again the terrible shriek rang out.

There was no mistaking the voice of the Skriker for that of anything else upon earth, and, with a sickly feeling at his heart, Adam slowly emerged from the gloom, and, in expectation of the appearance of the ghastly figure, passed on. He had not to wait long, for as he reached the old bridge spanning the Hodder, once more he saw, in the centre of the road, about midway of the stream, the same terrible object he had followed along the lane from the brook at Thornley.

With a sensation of terror somewhat less intense than that which had previously influenced him, he again yielded to the power which impelled him forward, and once more the strange procession commenced, the Skriker gliding over the snow, not, however, without a peculiar shuffling of its feet, surrounded, as they were, by masses of long hair, which clung to them, and deadened the sound, and Adam following in his mechanical and involuntary trot. The journey this time, however, was of but short duration, for the poor fellow's cottage was only a little way from the river. The distance was soon traversed, and the Skriker, with its face towards the terrified man, took up its position against the door of the dwelling. Adam could not resist the attraction which drew him to the ghastly thing, and as he neared it, in a fit of wild desperation, he struck at it, but his hand banged against the oak of the door, and, as the spectre splashed away, he fell forward in a swoon.

Disturbed by the noise of the fall, the goodwife arose and drew him into the cottage, but for some hours he was unable to tell the story of his terrible journey. When he had told of his involuntary chase of the Skriker, a deep gloom fell over the woman's features, for she well knew what the ghastly visit portended to their little household. The dread uncertainty did not continue long, however, for on the third day from that upon which Adam had reached his home the eldest lad was brought home drowned; and after attending the child's funeral, Adam's wife sickened of a fever, and within a few weeks she too was carried to Mytton churchyard. These things, together with the dreadful experience of the journey from Chipping, so affected Adam that he lost his reason, and for years afterwards the sound of his pattering footsteps, as in harmless idiotcy, with wild eyes and outstretched hands, he trotted along the roads in chase of an imaginary Boggart, fell with mournful impressiveness upon the ears of groups gathered by farm-house fires to listen to stories of the Skriker.{1}

THE UNBIDDEN GUEST.

In a little lane leading from the town of Clitheroe there once lived a
noted 'cunning man,' to whom all sorts of applications were made,
not only by the residents, but also by people from distant places, for
the fame of the wizard had spread over the whole country side. If a
theft was committed, at once the services of 'Owd Jeremy' were
enlisted, and, as a result, some one entirely innocent was, if not
accused, at least suspected; while maidens and young men,
anxious to pry into futurity, and behold the faces of their unknown
admirers, paid him trifling fees to enable them to gratify their
curiosity. In short, Jeremy professed to be an able student of the
Black Art, on familiar speaking terms with Satan, and duly qualified
to foretell men's destinies by the aid of the stars.

The cottage in which the old man resided was of a mean order, and
its outward appearance was by no means likely to impress visitors
with an idea that great pecuniary advantages had followed that
personal acquaintance with the Evil One of which the wizard
boasted. If, however, the outside was mean and shabby, the inside
of the dwelling was of a nature better calculated to inspire inquirers
with feelings of awe, hung round, as the one chamber was, with
faded and moth-eaten black cloth, upon which grotesque
astrological designs and the figure of a huge dragon were worked in
flaming red. The window being hidden by the dingy tapestry, the
only light in the room came from a starved-looking candle, which
was fixed in the foot of the skeleton of a child, attached to a string
from the ceiling, and dangling just over the table, where a
ponderous volume lay open before a large crystal globe and two
skulls.

In an old-fashioned chair, above which hung suspended a dirty and
dilapidated crocodile, the wizard sat, and gave audience to the
stray visitors whose desire to peer into futurity overmastered the fear
with which the lonely cottage was regarded. A quaint-looking old
man was Jeremy, with his hungry-looking eyes and long white
beard; and, as with bony fingers he turned over the leaves of the
large book, there was much in his appearance likely to give the
superstitious and ignorant customers overwhelming ideas of his
wondrous wisdom. The 'make up' was creditable to Jeremy, for
though he succeeded in deceiving others with his assumption of
supernatural knowledge, he himself did not believe in those powers
whose aid he so frequently professed to invoke on behalf of his

clients.

One day, when the ragged cloth had fallen behind a victim who was departing from the wizard's sanctum with a few vague and mysterious hints in exchange for solid coin, the old man, after laughing sarcastically, pulled aside the dingy curtains and stepped to the casement, through which the glorious sunlight was streaming. The scene upon which the wizard looked was a very beautiful one; and the old man leaned his head upon his hands and gazed intently upon the landscape.

"Tis a bonnie world,' said he,--"tis a bonnie world, and there are few views in it to compare with this one for beauty. My soul is drawn toward old Pendle, yon, with a love passing that of woman, heartless and passionless though the huge mass be. Heartless!' said he, after a pause,--'heartless! when every minute there is a fresh expression upon its beautiful front? Ay, even so, for it looms yonder calm and unconcerned when we are ushered into the world, and when we are ushered out of it, and laid to moulder away under the mountain's shadow; and it will rear its bold bluffs to heaven and smile in the sunlight or frown in the gloom after we who now love to gaze upon it are blind to the solemn loveliness of its impassable face. Poor perishable fools are we, with less power than the breeze which ruffles yon purple heather!'

With a heavy sigh Jeremy turned away from the window, and as the curtain fell behind him, and he stood again in the wretchedly-lighted room, he saw that he was not alone. The chair in which the trembling hinds generally were asked to seat themselves held a strange-looking visitor of dark and forbidding aspect.

'Jeremiah,' said this personage, 'devildom first and poetising afterwards.'

There was an unpleasant tone of banter in this speech, which did not seem in keeping with the character of one who fain would pry into futurity; and as the wizard took his usual position beneath the crocodile, he looked somewhat less oracular than was his wont when in front of a shivering and terrified inquirer.

'What wantest thou with me?' said he, with an ill-assumed appearance of unconcern.

The occupant of the chair smiled sardonically as he replied--

'A little security--that's all. For five-and-twenty years thou hast been amassing wealth by duping credulous fools, and it is time I had my percentage.'

The wizard stared in astonishment. Was the stranger a thief, or worse? he wondered, but after a time, however, he said, drily--

'Even if thou hadst proved thy right to a portion of the profits of my honest calling--and thou hast not--thou wouldst not require a packhorse to carry thy share away. Doth this hovel resemble the abode of a possessor of great wealth? Two chairs, a table, and a few old bones, its furniture; and its tenant a half-starved old man, who has had hard work to support life upon the pittance he receives in return for priceless words of wisdom! Thou art a stranger to me, and thy portion of my earnings is correctly represented by a circle.'

A loud and unmusical laugh followed the wizard's words; and before the unpleasant sound had died away the visitor remarked--

'If I am yet a stranger to thee, Jeremiah, 'tis not thy fault, for during the last quarter of a century thou hast boasted of me as thy willing servant, and extorted hard cash from thy customers upon the strength of my friendship and willingness to help thee; and now, true to thy beggarly instincts, thou wouldst deny me! But 'twill be in vain, Jeremiah--'twill be in vain! I have postponed this visit too long already to be put off with subterfuges now.'

'I repeat, I know thee not,' said the wizard, in a trembling voice. And, hurriedly rising from his chair, he flung aside the thick curtain, in order that the light of day might stream into the chamber, for a nameless fear had taken possession of him, and he did not care to remain in the darkened apartment with his suspicious visitor. To his surprise and terror, however, darkness had fallen upon the scene, and, as he gazed in alarm at the little diamond-framed window, through which so short a time before he had looked upon a fair prospect of meadow and mountain, a vivid flash of lightning darted across the heavens, and a clap of thunder burst over the cottage.

"Twill spoil good men's harvests, Jeremiah,' the stranger calmly said; 'but it need not interrupt our interesting conversation.'

Angry at the bantering manner in which the visitor spoke, the wizard flung open the door, and cried--

'Depart from my dwelling, ere I cast thee forth into the mire!'

'Surely thou wouldst not have the heart to fulfil thy threat,' said the stranger, 'although 'tis true I have but one shoe to be soiled by the mud.' And as he spoke he quietly crossed his legs, and Jeremiah perceived a hideous cloven foot.

With a groan, the wizard sank into his chair, and, deaf to the roaring of the thunder, and to the beating of the rain through the doorway, he sat helplessly gazing at his guest, whose metallic laughter rang through the room.

'Hast thou at length recognised me, Jeremiah?' asked the Evil One, after an interval, during which he had somewhat prominently displayed the hoof, and gloated over the agony its exhibition had caused his victim.

The old man was almost too terrified to answer, but at last he whispered--

'I have.'

'And thou no longer wilt refuse me the security?' hissed the tormentor, as he placed a parchment upon the table.

'What security dost thou demand?' feebly inquired the quaking wizard.

'Personal only,' said Satan. 'Put thy name to this,' and he pointed to the bond.

Jeremy pushed his chair as far from the suspicious-looking document as he could ere he replied--

'Thou shalt not have name of mine.'

He had expected that an outburst of fiendish wrath would follow this speech, but to his surprise the guest simply remarked--

'Very well, Jeremiah. By to-morrow night, however, thou shalt be exposed as the base and ignorant pretender thou art. Thou hast trespassed upon the rightful trade of my faithful servants long enough, and 'tis time I stopped thy prosperous career. Ere sunset thou shalt have a rival, who will take the bread from thy ungrateful mouth.'

After this polite speech the visitor picked up the parchment, and began to fold it in a methodical manner.

Such utterly unexpected gentlemanly behaviour somewhat reassured Jeremiah, and in a fainter voice he humbly asked what his visitor had to give in exchange for a wizard's autograph.

'Twenty-two years of such success as thou hast not even dared to dream of! No opposition--no exposure to thy miserable dupes,' readily answered Satan.

Jeremiah considered deeply. The offer undoubtedly was a tempting one, for after all, his profession had not been very lucrative, and to lose his customers, therefore, meant starvation. He was certain that if another wizard opened an establishment the people would flock to him, even through mere curiosity; but he knew what signing the bond included, and he was afraid to take the step.

After a long delay, during which Satan carefully removed a sharp stone from his hoof, Jeremiah therefore firmly said--

'Master, I'll not sign!'

Without more ado the visitor departed, and almost before he was out of sight the storm abated, and old Pendle again became visible.

A few days passed, and no one came to the dwelling of the wizard; and as such an absence of customers was very unusual, Jeremy began to fear that the supernatural stranger had not forgotten his threat. On the evening of the fifth day he crept into the little town to purchase some articles of food. Previously, whenever he had had occasion to make a similar journey, as he passed along the street the children ran away in terror, and the older people addressed him with remarkable humility; but this time, as he stepped rapidly past the houses, the youngsters went on with their games as though only an ordinary mortal went by, and a burly fellow who was leaning against a door jamb took his pipe from his mouth to cry familiarly--

'Well, Jerry, owd lad, heaw are ta'?'

These marks of waning power and fading popularity were sufficiently unmistakable; but as he was making his few purchases he was informed that a stranger, who seemed to be possessed of miraculous powers, had arrived in the town, and that many people who had been to him were going about testifying to his wonderful skill. With a heavy heart the wizard returned to his cottage. Next night a shower of stones dashed his window to pieces, and, as he peered into the moonlight lane, he saw a number of rough fellows, who evidently were waiting and watching in hopes that he would emerge from his dwelling. These were the only visitors he had during an entire week; and at length, quite prepared to capitulate, he said to himself--

'I wish I had another chance.'

No sooner had he uttered the words, than there was a sudden burst of thunder, wind roared round the house, again the clients' chair was occupied, and the parchment lay upon the table just as though it had not been disturbed.

'Art thou ready to sign?' asked Satan.

'Ay!' answered the old man.

The Evil One immediately seized the wizard's hand, upon which Jeremy gave a piercing yell, as well he might do, for the Satanic grip had forced the blood from the tips of his fingers.

'Sign!' said the Devil.

'I can't write,' said the wizard.

The Evil One forthwith took hold of one of the victim's fingers, and using it as a pen, wrote in a peculiarly neat hand 'Jeremiah Parsons, his × mark,' finishing with a fiendish flourish.

After doing this he again vacated the chair and the room as mysteriously as on the previous occasion.

The autograph-loving visitor had barely departed with the

parchment ere a knock at the door was heard, and in stepped a man who wished to have the veil lifted, and who brought the pleasing news that, influenced by the reports of the opposition wizard, he had been to his house in Clitheroe, but had found it empty, the whilom tenant having fled no one knew whither. From that time things looked up with Jeremy, and money poured into the skulls, for people crowded from far and near to test his skill. For two-and-twenty years he flourished and was famous, but the end came.{2} One morning, after a wild night when the winds howled round Pendle, and it seemed as though all the powers of darkness were let loose, some labourers who were going to their work were surprised to find only the ruins of the wizard's cottage. The place had been consumed by fire; and although search was made for the magician's remains, only a few charred bones were found, and these, some averred, were not those of old Jeremy, but were relics of the dusty old skeleton and the dirty crocodile under the shadow of which the wizard used to sit.

THE FAIRY'S SPADE.

'Th' fairies han getten varra shy sin' thee an' me wir young, Matty, lass!' said an old grey-headed man, who, smoking a long pipe, calmly sat in a shady corner of the kitchen of a Fylde country farm-house. 'Nubry seems to see 'em neaw-a-days as they ust. I onst had a seet o' one on 'em, as plain as I con see thee sittin' theer, ravellin' thi owd stockin'. I wir ploughin' varra soon after dayleet, an' ther worn't a saand to be heeart nobbut th' noise o'th' graand oppenin', an' th' chirp ov a few brids wakkenin' an' tunin' up, an' ov a toothrey crows close at after mi heels a-pikin' up th' whorms. O ov a suddent I heeard sumbry cry, i' a voice like owd Luke wench i'th' orgin loft ov a Sundays, "I've brokken mi speet!" I lost no toime i' tornin' to see whoa wir at wark at that haar, an' i' aar fielt too, an' I clapt mi een on as pratty a little lass as ever oppent een i' this country side. Owd England choilt's bonny, yone warrant mi, but hoo's as feaw as sin aside o'th' face as I see that morn. Hoo stood theer wi' th' brokken spade i' her hond, an' i'th' tother a hommer an' a toothrey nails, an' hoo smoilt at mi, an' offert mi th' tackle, as mich as t' say, "Naaw, Isik, be gradely for onst i' thi loife, an' fettle this speet for mi, will ta?" For a whoile I stood theear gapin' like a foo', and wontherin' wheear hoo could ha' risen fray, but hoo cried aat onst mooar, "I've brokken mi speet!" Sooa I marcht toart her and tuk th' hommer an' th' nails, an' tacklet it up. It didn't tek mi long a-dooin', for it wir but a loile un; but when I'd done hoo smoilt at mi, an' so bonny, summat loike tha ust, Margit, when owd Pigheeod wir cooartin' tha; an' gan mi a hanful o' brass,{3} an' afooar I'd time to say owt off hoo vanisht. That wur th' only feorin as ivver I've seen, an' mebbi th' only one as I'm likely to luk at, for mi seet's getten nooan o'th' best latterly.

THE KING OF THE FAIRIES.

Many years ago there lived in a farm-house at a point of the high-
road from Manchester to Stockport, where Levenshulme Church
now stands, a worthy named Burton, 'Owd Dannel Burton.'[A] The
farm held by Daniel was a model one in its way, the old man raising
finer crops than any other farmer in the district. It was rumoured that
Daniel was very comfortably provided for, and that a few bad years
would not harm him; and so wonderfully did everything he took in
hand prosper, that his 'luck' became proverbial. Such uniform
prosperity could not long continue without the tongue of envy and
detraction being set wagging, and the neighbours who permitted
thistles to overrun their pastures whilst they gadded about to rush-
bearings and wakes, finding a reproach to their idleness not only in
the old man's success, but also in the careful, industrious habits of his
daily life, were not slow to insinuate that there was something more
than farming at the bottom of it. 'Dannel' had sold himself to Satan,
said some whose pigs had faded away, and whose harvests had
not been worth the gathering; and others pretended to know even
the terms of the contract, and how many years the old man yet had
to play on. A few of these detractors were young men whose
imaginations were not kept in sufficient control, but they grew
wonderfully reserved respecting the Satanic bargain after the hearty
Daniel had had an interview with them, and proved to them that he
had not forgotten the use of a good tough black-thorn.

[A] Mr. Burton's grandson was for many years rector of All Saints',
Manchester.

'It's nobbut luck,' philosophically remarked others, 'mebbe it'll be my
turn to-morn;' but the remainder vowed that neither luck or Evil One
had anything to do with it, for the success was due to the labours of
Puck, King of the Fairies.

They were right. It was Puck, although no one ever knew how the
old man had been able to enlist the services of so valuable an
auxiliary, Daniel being strangely reticent upon the point, although
generally by no means loth to speak of the fairies and their doings.
Reserve with reference to these things, however, would not have
availed much, for the farm labourers, the ruddy-cheeked milkmaids,
and the other women-folk about the farm-house, were fond of
boasting of the exploits of Puck--how during the night everything
was 'cleaned up,' and all was in apple-pie order when they came

into the kitchen at daybreak, the milk churned, the cows foddered, the necessary utensils filled with water from the well, the horses ready harnessed for their day's work at the plough, and even a week's threshing done and the barn left as tidy as though it had just been emptied and swept. Evidently the servant lasses had no fear of, or objection to, a hard-working supernatural visitor of this kind, but just the reverse, and many of their listeners found themselves wishing that their house, too, had its Boggart.

For so long a period did this state of things continue, each morning revealing an astounding amount of work performed by the willing and inexpensive workman, that at length the assistance was taken for granted, and as a matter of course, offering no food for surprise, although it did not cease to be a cause of envy to the neighbours.

On one occasion, however, as old Daniel was despatching a hearty and substantial breakfast, a heated labourer brought word that all the corn had been housed during the past night. The strange story was true enough, for when the old man reached the field, where on the previous evening the golden sheaves of wheat had stood, he found the expanse quite bare, and as clean as though reapers, leaders, gleaners, and geese had been carefully over it. The harvest was in the barn, but not content with this, Daniel, illustrating the old proverb that 'much would have more,' suddenly exclaimed, 'I wonder whose horses Puck{4} used in this work. If yon of mine, I daresay he sweated them rarely;' and away he strode towards the stable. He had not reached the fold, however, when he met Puck coming towards him, and in a fever of greedy anxiety he cried, 'Puck, I doubt thou'st spoiled yon horses!' No sooner were the words out of his mouth, however, than he saw that for once in his life he had made a mistake, for the fairy went pale with anger as he shouted in a shrill treble:--Sheaf to field, and horse to stall,I, the Fairy King, recall!Never more shall drudge of mineStir a horse or sheaf of thine.

After which vow he at once vanished.

The old man walked home in a sorrowful mood, and actually forgot to go to the stable; but next morning early he was disturbed by a knocking at his chamber door. 'Mesthur, ger up,' cried the messenger, who on the previous day had brought the news of the housing of the corn, 'Mesthur, ger up, th' corn's back i'th' fielt.' With a groan of anguish Daniel arose, and hastily made his way to the barn. All the pile was gone, and the floor littered with straw, exactly as it was before the fairy labour had so transformed the place.

It did not take the farmer long to get over the ground between his barn and the corn-field, and arrived there he found the expanse once more covered with yellow sheaves, on which the beams of the rising sun were beginning to fall. Here and there a sheaf had fallen upon the ground, and everywhere straw and ears of corn were scattered about as though the reapers had not long before left the place. The old man turned away in despair.

From that time forward there was no more work done about the farm, or the shippons, and stables; but in the house, however, the maids continued to find their tasks performed as usual.

Great were the rejoicings in the locality when the story of the sheaves became known, and it got noised about that 'Dannel's' fairy had 'fown eawt' with him. The old man became very dejected, for although he did not clearly perceive that the rupture was entirely due to his own selfish greed, he could not go about the farm without observing how much he had lost.

One summer evening in a thoughtful mood he was walking homewards, and wishing that the meadows were mown. Plunged in such reflections, he met a neighbour, who at once asked the cause of his trouble. Daniel turned to point to the meadows, and as he did so he saw the fairy, in an attitude of rapt attention, stooping behind the hedgerow as though anxious to overhear the conversation. 'Yo' miss your neet-mon?' said the neighbour. The old man thought that the time was come to make his peace with offended royalty, and with a cunning glance in the direction of the hiding-place, he answered, 'I do, Abrum, and may God bless Puck, th' King o'th' Fayrees.'{5} There was a startled cry from behind the hedgerow, and both men turned in that direction, but there was nothing to be observed. The fairy had vanished, never again to be seen in Daniel Burton's fields. That night the work was left undone even inside the farm-house, and thenceforward when the kitchen needed cleaning, water was wanted from the well, or when milk had to be churned, the maids had to get up early and do the work, for Puck, King of the Fairies, would not touch either mop or pail.

MOTHER AND CHILD.

The tenants of Plumpton Hall had retired to rest somewhat earlier than was their wont, for it was the last night of November.

The old low rooms were in darkness, and all was silent as the grave; for though the residents, unfortunately for themselves, were not asleep, they held their breath, and awaited in fear the first stroke of the hour from the old clock in the kitchen. Suddenly the sound of hurried footsteps broke the silence; but with sighs of relief the terrified listeners found that the noise was made by a belated wayfarer, almost out of his wits with fright, but who was unable to avoid passing the hall, and who, therefore, ran by the haunted building as quickly as his legs could carry him. The sensation of escape, however, was of but short duration, for the hammer commenced to strike; and no sooner had the last stroke of eleven startled the echoes than loud thuds, as of a heavy object bumping upon the stairs, were heard.

The quaking occupants of the chambers hid their heads beneath the bedclothes, for they knew that an old-fashioned oak chair was on its way down the noble staircase, and was sliding from step to step as though dragged along by an invisible being who had only one hand at liberty.

If any one had dared to follow that chair across the wide passage and into the wainscoted parlour, he would have been startled by the sight of a fire blazing in the grate, whence, ere the servants retired, even the very embers had been removed, and in the chair, the marvellous movement of which had so frightened all the inmates of the hall, he would have seen a beautiful woman seated, with an infant at her breast.

Year after year, on wild nights, when the snow was driven against the diamond panes, and the cry of the spirit of the storm came up from the sea, the weird firelight shone from the haunted room, and through the house sounded a mysterious crooning as the unearthly visitor softly sang a lullaby to her infant. Lads grew up into grey-headed men in the old house; and from youth to manhood, on the last night of each November, they had heard the notes, but none of them ever had caught, even when custom had somewhat deadened the terror which surrounded the events of the much-dreaded anniversary, the words of the song the ghostly woman sang. The maids, too, had always found the grate as it was left before the visit--not a cinder or speck of dust remaining to tell of the strange fire, and no one had ever heard the chair ascend the stairs. Chair and fire and child and mother, however, were seen by many a weary wayfarer, drawn to the house by the hospitable look of the window, through which the genial glow of the burning logs shone forth into the night, but who, by tapping at the pane and crying for shelter, could not attract the attention of the pale nurse, clad in a quaint old costume with lace ruff and ruffles, and singing a mournful and melodious lullaby to the child resting upon her beautiful bosom.

Tradition tells of one of these wanderers, a footsore and miserable seafaring man on the tramp, who, attracted by the welcome glare, crept to the panes, and seeing the cosy-looking fire, and the Madonna-faced mother tenderly nursing her infant, rapped at the glass and begged for a morsel of food and permission to sleep in the hayloft--and, finding his pleadings unanswered, loudly cursed the woman who could sit and enjoy warmth and comfort and turn a deaf ear to the prayers of the homeless and hungry; upon which the seated figure turned the weird light of its wild eyes upon him and almost changed him to stone--a labourer, going to his daily toil in the early morn, finding the poor wretch gazing fixedly through the window, against which his terror-stricken face was closely pressed, his hair turned white by fear, and his fingers convulsively clutching the casement.

THE SPECTRAL CAT.

Long ago--so long, in fact, that the date has been lost in obscurity--
the piously-inclined inhabitants of the then thickly wooded and wild
country stretching from the sea-coast to Rivington Pike and Hoghton
determined to erect a church at Whittle-le-Woods, and a site having
been selected, the first stone was laid with all the ceremony due to
so important and solemn a proceeding. Assisted by the labours as
well as by the contributions of the faithful, the good priest was in
high spirits; and as the close of the first day had seen the
foundations set out and goodly piles of materials brought upon the
ground ready for the future, he fell asleep congratulating himself
upon having lived long enough to see the wish of his heart gratified.
What was his surprise, however, when, after arising at the break of
day, and immediately rushing to his window to gaze upon the work,
he could not perceive either foundation or pile of stone, the field in
which he expected to observe the promising outline being as green
and showing as few marks of disturbance as the neighbouring
ones.{6}

'Surely I must have been dreaming,' said the good man, as he stood
with rueful eyes at the little casement, 'for there are not any signs
either of the gifts or the labours of the pious sons of the church.'

In this puzzled frame of mind, and with a heavy sigh, he once more
courted sleep. He had not slumbered long, however, when loud
knocks at the door of his dwelling and lusty cries for Father Ambrose
disturbed him. Hastily attiring himself, he descended, to find a
concourse of people assembled in front of the house; and no sooner
had he opened the door than a mason cried out--

'Father Ambrose, where are the foundations we laid yesterday, and
where is the stone from the quarry?'

'Then I did not simply dream that I had blessed the site?' said the old
man, inquiringly.

Upon which there was a shout of laughter, and a sturdy young
fellow asked--

'And I did not dream that I carted six loads from the quarry?'

'Th' Owd Lad's hed a hand int',' said a labourer, 'for t' fielt's as if fuut

---

hed never stept int'.'

The priest and his people at once set off to inspect the site, and sure enough it was in the state described by the mason; cowslips and buttercups decking the expanse of green, which took different shades as the zephyr swept over it.

'Well, I'm fair capped,' said a grey-headed old farmer. 'I've hed things stown afoor today, bud they'n generally bin things wi' feathers on an' good to heyt an' not th' feaundations uv a church. Th' warlt's gerrin' ter'ble wickit. We's hev' to bi lukkin' eawt for another Noah's flood, I warrant.'

A peal of laughter followed this sally, but Father Ambrose, who was in no mood for mirth, sternly remarked--'There is something here which savoureth of the doings of Beelzebub;' and then he sadly turned away, leaving the small crowd of gossips speculating upon the events of the night. Before the father reached his dwelling, however, he heard his name called by a rustic who was running along the road.

'Father Ambrose,' cried the panting messenger, 'here's the strangest thing happened at Leyland. The foundations of a church and all sorts of building materials have been laid in a field during the night, and Adam the miller is vowing vengeance against you for having trespassed on his land.'

The priest at once returned to the little crowd of people, who still were gaping at the field from which all signs of labour had been so wonderfully removed, and bade the messenger repeat the strange story, which he did at somewhat greater length, becoming loquacious in the presence of his equals, for he enjoyed their looks of astonishment. When the astounding narrative had been told, the crowd at once started for Leyland, their pastor promising to follow after he had fortified himself with breakfast.

When the good man reached the village he had no need to inquire which was Adam the miller's field, for he saw the crowd gathered in a rich-looking meadow. As he opened the gate Adam met him, and without ceremony at once accused him of having taken possession of his field. 'Peace, Adam,' said the priest. 'The field hath been taken not by me, but by a higher power, either good or evil--I fear the latter,' and he made his way to the people. True enough,

the foundations were laid as at Whittle, and even the mortar was
ready for the masons. 'I am loth to think that this is a sorry jest of the
Evil One,' said Father Ambrose; 'ye must help me to outwit him, and
to give him his labour for his pains. Let each one carry what he can,
and, doubtless, Adam will be glad to cart the remainder,'--a
proposition the burly miller agreed to at once. Accordingly each of
the people walked off with a piece of wood, and Adam started for
his team. Before long the field was cleared, and ere sunset the
foundations were again laid in the original place, and a goodly
piece of wall had been built.

Grown wise by experience, the priest selected two men to watch
the place during the night. Naturally enough, these worthies, who by
no means liked the task, but were afraid to decline it, determined to
make themselves as comfortable as they could under the
circumstances.

They therefore carried to the place a quantity of food and drink,
and a number of empty sacks, with which they constructed an
impromptu couch near the blazing wood fire. Notwithstanding the
seductive influence of the liquor, they were not troubled with much
company, for the few people who resided in the vicinity did not
care to remain out of doors late after what Father Ambrose had said
as to the proceeding having been a joke of Satan's. The priest,
however, came to see the men, and after giving them his blessing,
and a few words of advice, he left them to whatever the night
might bring forth. No sooner had he gone than the watchers put up
some boards to shield them from the wind, and, drawing near to the
cheerful fire, they began to partake of a homely but plentiful
supper. Considering how requisite it was that they should be in
possession of all their wits, perhaps it would have been better had
not a large bottle been in such frequent requisition, for, soon after
the meal was ended, what with the effects of the by-no-means
weak potion, the warmth and odour sent forth by the crackling logs,
and the musical moaning of the wind in the branches overhead,
they began to feel drowsy, to mutter complaints against the
hardship of their lot, and to look longingly upon the heap of sacks.

'If owt comes,' said the oldest of the two, 'one con see it as well as
two, an' con wakken t' tother--theerfore I'm in for a nod.' And he at
once flung himself upon the rude bed.

'Well,' said the younger one, who was perched upon a log close to the fire, 'hev thi own way, an' tha'll live lunger; but I'se wakken tha soon, an' hev a doze mysen. That's fair, isn't it?'

To this question there was no response, for the old man was already asleep. The younger one immediately reached the huge bottle, and after drinking a hearty draught from it placed it within reach, saying, as he did so--

'I'm nooan freetunt o' thee, as heaw it is! Thaart not Belsybub, are ta?'

Before long he bowed his head upon his hands, and gazing into the fire gave way to a pleasant train of reflections, in which the miller's daughter played a by-no-means unimportant part. In a little while he, too, began to doze and nod, and the ideas and thronging fancies soon gave way to equally delightful dreams.

Day was breaking when the pair awoke; the fire was out, and the noisy birds were chirping their welcome to the sun. For a while the watchers stared at each other with well-acted surprise.

'I'm freetunt tha's o'erslept thysel',' said the young fellow; 'and rayly I do think as I've bin noddin' a bit mysen.' And then, as he turned round, 'Why, it's gone ageean! Jacob, owd lad! th' foundation, an' th' wo's, an' o th' lots o' stooans are off t' Leyland ageean!'

The field was again clear, grass and meadow flowers covering its expanse, and after a long conference the pair determined that the best course for them to pursue would be that of immediately confessing to Father Ambrose that they had been asleep. Accordingly they wended their way to his house, and having succeeded in arousing him, and getting him to the door, the young man informed him that once more the foundations were missing.

'What took them?' asked the priest. To which awkward query the old man replied, that they did not see anything.

'Then ye slept, did ye?' asked the Father.

'Well,' said the young man, 'we did nod a minnit or two; but we wir toired wi' watchin' so closely; an', yo' see, that as con carry th' foundations ov a church away connot hev mich trouble i' sendin' unlarnt chaps loike Jacob an' me to sleep agen eaur will.'

This ended the colloquy, for Father Ambrose laughed heartily at the ready answer. Shortly afterwards, as on the preceding day, the messenger from Leyland arrived with tidings that the walls had again appeared in Adam's field. Again they were carted back, and placed in their original position, and once more was a watch set, the priest taking the precaution of remaining with the men until near upon midnight. Almost directly after he had left the field one of the watchers suddenly started from his seat, and cried--

'See yo', yonder, there's summat wick!'

Both men gazed intently, and saw a huge cat, with great unearthly-looking eyes, and a tail with a barbed end. Without any seeming difficulty this terrible animal took up a large stone, and hopped off with it, returning almost immediately for another. This strange performance went on for some time, the two observers being nearly petrified by terror; but at length the younger one said--

'I'm like to put a stop to yon wark, or hee'll say win bin asleep ageean,' and seizing a large piece of wood he crept down the field, the old man following closely behind. When he reached the cat, which took no notice of his approach, he lifted his cudgel, and struck the animal a heavy blow on its head. Before he had time to repeat it, however, the cat, with a piercing scream, sprang upon him, flung him to the ground, and fixed its teeth in his throat. The old man at once fled for the priest. When he returned with him, cat, foundations, and materials were gone; but the dead body of the poor watcher was there, with glazed eyes, gazing at the pitiless stars.

After this terrible example of the power of the fiendish labourer it was not considered advisable to attempt a third removal, and the building was proceeded with upon the site at Leyland chosen by the spectre.

The present parish church covers the place long occupied by the original building; and although all the actors in this story passed away centuries ago, a correct likeness of the cat has been preserved, and may be seen by the sceptical.{7}

THE CAPTURED FAIRIES.

There once lived in the little village of Hoghton two idle, good-for-nothing fellows, who, somehow or other, managed to exist without spending the day, from morn to dewy eve, at the loom. When their more respectable neighbours were hard at work they generally were to be seen either hanging about the doorway of the little ale-house or playing at dominoes inside the old-fashioned hostelry; and many a time in broad daylight their lusty voices might be heard as they trolled forth the hearty poaching ditty,'It's my delight, on a shiny night.'

It was understood that they had reason to sympathise with the sentiments expressed in the old ballad. Each was followed by a ragged, suspicious-looking lurcher; and as the four lounged about the place steady-going people shook their heads, and prophesied all sorts of unpleasant terminations to so unsatisfactory a career. So far as the dogs were concerned the dismal forebodings were verified, for from poaching in the society of their masters the clever lurchers took to doing a little on their own account, and both were shot in the pursuit of game by keepers, who were only too glad of an opportunity of ridding the neighbourhood of such misdirected intelligence. Soon after this unfortunate event, the two men, who themselves had a narrow escape, had their nets taken; and, as they were too poor to purchase others, and going about to borrow such articles was equivalent to accusing their friends of poaching habits, they were reduced to the necessity of using sacks whenever they visited the squire's fields.

One night, after climbing the fence and making their way to a well-stocked warren, they put in a solitary ferret and rapidly fixed the sacks over the burrows. They did not wait long in anxious expectation of an exodus before there was a frantic rush, and after hastily grasping the sacks tightly round the necks, and tempting their missionary from the hole, they crept through the hedgerow, and at a sharp pace started for home. For some time they remained unaware of the nature of their load, and they were congratulating themselves upon the success which had crowned their industry, when suddenly there came a cry from one of the prisoners, 'Dick, wheer art ta?' The poachers stood petrified with alarm; and almost immediately a voice from the other bag piped out--'In a sack,On a back,Riding up Hoghton Brow.'{8}

The terrified men at once let their loads fall, and fled at the top of their speed, leaving behind them the bags full of fairies, who had been driven from their homes by the intruding ferret. Next morning, however, the two poachers ventured to the spot where they had heard the supernatural voices. The sacks neatly folded were lying at the side of the road, and the men took them up very tenderly, as though in expectation of another mysterious utterance, and crept off with them.

Need it be said that those bags were not afterwards used for any purpose more exciting than the carriage of potatoes from the previously neglected bit of garden, the adventure having quite cured the men of any desire to 'pick up' rabbits.

Like most sudden conversions, however, that of the two poachers into hard-working weavers was regarded with suspicion by the inhabitants of the old-world village, and in self-defence the whilom wastrels were forced to tell the story of the imprisonment of the fairies. The wonderful narrative soon got noised abroad; and as the changed characters, on many a summer evening afterwards, sat hard at work in their loom-house, and, perhaps almost instinctively, hummed the old ditty,'It's my delight, on a shiny night,'

the shock head of a lad would be protruded through the honeysuckle which almost covered the casement, as the grinning youngster, who had been patiently waiting for the weaver to commence his song and give an opportunity for the oft-repeated repartee, cried, 'Nay, it isn't thi delight; "Dick, wheer art ta?"'

THE PILLION LADY.

It was on a beautiful night in the middle of summer that Humphrey Dobson, after having transacted a day's business at Garstang market, and passed some mirthful hours with a number of jovial young fellows in the best parlour of the Ffrances Arms, with its oak furniture and peacock feathers, mounted his steady-going mare, and set off for home. He had got some distance from the little town, and was rapidly nearing a point where the road crossed a stream said to be haunted by the spirit of a female who had been murdered many years back; and although the moon was shining brightly, and the lonely rider could see far before him, there was one dark spot overshadowed by trees a little in advance which Humphrey feared to reach. He felt a thrill of terror as he suddenly remembered the many strange stories told of the headless woman whose sole occupation and delight seemed to be that of terrifying travellers; but, with a brave endeavour to laugh off his fears, he urged his horse forward, and attempted to troll forth the burden of an old song:--'He rode and he rode till he came to the dooar,And Nell came t' oppen it, as she'd done afooar:"Come, get off thy horse," she to him did say,"An' put it i'th' stable, an' give it some hay."'

It would not do, however; and suddenly he put spurs to the mare and galloped towards the little bridge. No sooner did the horse's hoofs ring upon the stones than Humphrey heard a weird and unearthly laugh from beneath the arch, and, as the animal snorted and bounded forward, the young fellow felt an icy arm glide round his waist and a light pressure against his back. Drops of perspiration fell from his brow, and his heart throbbed wildly, but he did not dare to look behind lest his worst fears should be verified, and he should behold 'th' boggart o'th' bruk.'

As though conscious of its ghastly burden, the old mare ran as she never had run before; the hedgerows and trees seemed to fly past, while sparks streamed from the flints in the road, and in an incredibly short space of time the farm-house was reached. Instinctively, Humphrey tried to guide the mare into the yard, but his efforts were powerless, for the terrified animal had got the bit in her teeth, and away she sped past the gateway.

As the rider was thus borne away, another sepulchral laugh broke the silence, but this time it sounded so close to the horseman's ear that he involuntarily looked round.

He found that the figure, one of whose arms was twined round his waist, was not the headless being of whom he had heard so many fearful narratives, but another and a still more terrible one, for, grinning in a dainty little hood, and almost touching his face, there was a ghastly skull, with eyeless sockets, and teeth gleaming white in the clear moonlight.

Petrified by fear, he could not turn his head away, and, as the mare bore him rapidly along, ever and anon a horrid derisive laugh sounded in his ears as for a moment the teeth parted and then closed with a sudden snap. Terrified as he was, however, he noticed that the arm which encircled his body gradually tightened around him, and putting down his hand to grasp it he found it was that of a fleshless skeleton.

How long he rode thus embraced by a spectre he knew not, but it seemed an age.

Suddenly, however, as at a turn in the road the horse stumbled and fell, Humphrey, utterly unprepared for any such occurrence, was thrown over the animal's head and stunned by the fall.

When he recovered full consciousness it was daybreak. The sun was rising, the birds were singing in the branching foliage overhead, and the old mare was quietly grazing at a distance. With great difficulty, for he was faint through loss of blood, and lame, he got home and told his story. There were several stout men about the farm who professed to disbelieve it, and pretended to laugh at the idea of a skeleton horsewoman, who, without saying with your leave or by your leave, had ridden pillion with the young master, but it was somewhat remarkable that none of them afterwards could be induced to cross the bridge over the haunted stream after 'th' edge o' dark.

'THE FAIRY FUNERAL.

There are few spots in Lancashire more likely to have been peopled by fairies than that portion of the highway which runs along the end of Penwortham wood.

At all times the locality is very beautiful, but it is especially so in summer, when the thin line of trees on the one side of the road and the rustling wood upon the other cast a welcome shade upon the traveller, who can rest against the old railings, and look down upon a rich expanse of meadow-land and corn-fields, bounded in the distance by dim, solemn-looking hills, and over the white farm-houses, snugly set in the midst of luxurious vegetation. From this vantage-ground a flight of steps leads down to the well of St. Mary, the water of which, once renowned for its miraculous efficacy, is as clear as crystal and of never-ceasing flow.

To this sacred neighbourhood thousands of pilgrims have wended their way; and although the legend of the holy well has been lost, it is easy to understand with what superstitious reverence the place would be approached by those whose faith was of a devout and unquestioning kind, and what feelings would influence those whose hearts were heavy with the weight of a great sorrow as they descended the steps worn by the feet of their countless predecessors.

From the little spring a pathway winds across meadows and through corn-fields to the sheltered village, and a little further along the highway a beautiful avenue winds from the old lodge gates to the ancient church and priory. Wide as is this road it is more than shaded by the tall trees which tower on each side, their topmost branches almost interlaced, the sunbeams passing through the green network, and throwing fantastic gleams of light upon the pathway, along which so many have been carried to the quiet God's Acre.

At the end of this long and beautiful walk stands the old priory, no longer occupied by the Benedictines from Evesham, the silvery sound of whose voices at eventide used to swell across the rippling Ribble; and, a little to the right of the pile, the Church of St. Mary, with its background of the Castle Hill.

By the foot of this Ancient British and Roman outlook there is a little

---

farm-house, with meadow land stretching away to the broad river; and one night, fifty or sixty years ago, two men, one of whom was a local 'cow-doctor,' whose duties had compelled him to remain until a late hour, set out from this dwelling to walk home to the straggling village of Longton. It was near upon midnight when they stepped forth, but it was as light as mid-day, the moon shining in all her beauty, and casting her glamour upon the peaceful scene. So quiet was it that it seemed as though even the Zephyrs were asleep. There was not a breath of wind, and not a leaf rustled or a blade of grass stirred, and had it not been for the sounds of the footsteps of the two men, who were rapidly ascending the rough cart-track winding up the side of the hill, all would have been as still as death. The sweet silence was a fitting one, for in the graveyard by the side of the lane through which the travellers were passing, and over the low moss-covered wall of which might be seen the old-fashioned tombstones, erect like so many sentinels marking the confines of the battle-field of life, hundreds were sleeping the sleep with which only the music of the leaves, the sough of the wind, and the sigh of the sea seem in harmony.

As the two men opened the gate at the corner of the churchyard, the old clock sounded the first stroke of midnight.

'That's twelve on 'em,' said the oldest of the two.

'Ay, Adam,' said the other, a taller and much younger man. 'Another day's passin' away, an' it con't dee wi'eaut tellin' everybody; yet ther's bod few on us as tez onny notice on't, for we connot do to be towd as wer toime's growin' bod short. I should think as tha dusn't care to hear th' clock strike, Adam, to judge bith' colour o' thi toppin', for tha 'rt gerrin' varra wintry lookin'.'

The old man chuckled at this sally, and then said, slowly and drily:--

'Speyk for thisen, Robin--speyk for thisen; an' yet why should ta speyk at o? Choilt as tha are--an' tha art nobbut a choilt, clivver as tha fancies thisen--tha 'rt owd enough to mind as it's nod olus th' grey-heeoded uns as dees th' fost. Th' chickins fo' off th' peeark mooar oftener nor th' owd brids. Ther's monny an owd tree wi' nobbud a twothree buds o' green abaat it, to show as it wur yung wonst, as tha'd hev herd wark to delve up, th' roots bein' so deep i'th' graand; an' ther's monny a rook o' young-lukkin' uns as tha met poo up as yezzy as a hondful o' sallet. It teks leetnin' to kill th' owd oak, but th' fost nippin' woint off th' Martch yon soon puts th' bonnie spring posies out o' seet. If I'm growin' owd, let's hope I'm roipnin' as weel. Tha'rt not th' fost bit of a lad as thowt heer baan to last o th' tothers aat, an' as hed hardly toime to finish his crowin' afoor th' sexton clapt o honful o' sond i' his meauth.'

This conversation brought the two beyond the gate and some distance along the avenue, in which the moonlight was somewhat toned by the thickness of the foliage above, and they were rapidly nearing the lodge gates, when suddenly the solemn sound of a deep-toned bell broke the silence. Both men stopped and listened intently.

'That's th' passin'-bell,'{9} said Adam. 'Wodever con be up? I never knew it rung at this toime o'th' neet afooar.'

'Mek less racket, will ta,' said Robin. 'Led's keep count an' see heaw owd it is.'

Whilst the bell chimed six-and-twenty both listeners stood almost breathless, and then Adam said:--

'He's thy age, Robin, chuz who he is.'

'Ther wer no leet i 'th' belfry as wi come by, as I see on,' said the young man, 'I'd rayther be i' bed nor up theer towlin' ad this toime, wudn't tha?'

'Yoi,' said Adam. 'But owd Jemmy dusn't care, an' why should he? Hee's bin amung th' deeod to' long to be freet'nt on 'em neet or day, wake an' fable as he is. I dar' say hee's fun aat afoor neaw as they'r not varra rough to dale wi'. Ther's nod mich feightin i'th' bury-hoyle, beaut ids wi' th' resurrectioners. Bud led's get to'art whoam, lad; we're loikely enough to larn o abaat it to-morn.'

Without more words they approached the lodge, but to their great terror, when they were within a few yards from the little dwelling, the gates noiselessly swung open, the doleful tolling of the passing-bell being the only sound to be heard. Both men stepped back affrighted as a little figure clad in raiment of a dark hue, but wearing a bright red cap, and chanting some mysterious words in a low musical voice as he walked, stepped into the avenue.

'Ston back, mon,' cried Adam, in a terrified voice--'ston back; it's th' feeorin; bud they'll not hort tha if tha dusna meddle wi' um.'

The young man forthwith obeyed his aged companion, and standing together against the trunk of a large tree, they gazed at the miniature being stepping so lightly over the road, mottled by the stray moonbeams. It was a dainty little object; but although neither Adam nor Robin could comprehend the burden of the song it sang, the unmistakable croon of grief with which each stave ended told the listeners that the fairy was singing a requiem. The men kept perfectly silent, and in a little while the figure paused and turned round, as though in expectation, continuing, however, its mournful notes. By-and-by the voices of other singers were distinguished, and as they grew louder the fairy standing in the roadway ceased to render the verse, and sang only the refrain, and a few minutes afterwards Adam and Robin saw a marvellous cavalcade pass through the gateway. A number of figures, closely resembling the one to which their attention had first been drawn, walked two by two, and behind them others with their caps in their hands, bore a little black coffin, the lid of which was drawn down so as to leave a portion of the contents uncovered. Behind these again others, walking in pairs, completed the procession. All were singing in inexpressibly mournful tones, pausing at regular intervals to allow the voice of the one in advance to be heard, as it chanted the refrain of the song, and when the last couple had passed into the avenue, the gates closed as noiselessly as they had opened.

As the bearers of the burden marched past the two watchers, Adam bent down, and, by the help of a stray gleam of moonlight, saw that there was a little corpse in the coffin.

'Robin, mi lad,' said he, in a trembling voice and with a scared look, 'it's th' pictur o' thee as they hev i' th' coffin!'

With a gasp of terror the young man also stooped towards the bearers, and saw clearly enough that the face of the figure borne by the fairies indeed closely resembled his own, save that it was ghastly with the pallor and dews of death.

The procession had passed ere he was able to speak, for, already much affrighted by the appearance of the fairies, the sight of the little corpse had quite unnerved him. Clinging in a terrified manner to the old man, he said, in a broken voice--

---

'It raley wor me, Adam! Dust think it's a warnin', an' I'm abaat to dee?'

The old man stepped out into the road as he replied--

'It wur a quare seet, Robin, no daat; bud I've sin monny sich i' mi toime, an' theyne come to nowt i' th' end. Warnin' or not, haaever,' he added, with strong common sense, 'ther'll be no harm done bi thee livin' as if it wur one.'

The mournful music of the strange singers and the solemn sound of the passing bell could still be heard, and the two awe-struck men stood gazing after the cavalcade.

'It mon be a warnin', again said Robin, 'an' I wish I'd axed um haa soon I've to dee. Mebbee they'n a towd me.'

'I don't think they wod,' said Adam. 'I've olus heeard as they'r rare and vext if they'r spokken to. Theyn happen a done tha some lumberment if tha 'ad axed owt.'

'They could but a kilt mi,' replied Robin, adding, with that grim humour which so often accompanies despair, 'an' they're buryin' mi neaw, ar'nod they?' Then in a calm and firm voice he said--'I'm baan to ax 'em, come wod will. If tha 'rt freetent tha con goo on whoam.'

'Nay, nay,' said Adam warmly, 'I'm nooan scaret. If tha'rt for catechoizing um, I'll see th' end on it.'

Without further parley the men followed after and soon overtook the procession, which was just about to enter the old churchyard, the gates of which, like those of the lodge, swung open apparently of their own accord, and no sooner did Robin come up with the bearers than, in a trembling voice, he cried--

'Winnot yo' tell mi haaw lung I've to live?'

There was not any answer to this appeal, the little figure in front continuing to chant its refrain with even deepened mournfulness. Imagining that he was the leader of the band, Robin stretched out his hand and touched him. No sooner had he done this than, with startling suddenness, the whole cavalcade vanished, the gates banged to with a loud clang, deep darkness fell upon everything, the wind howled and moaned round the church and the tombstones in the graveyard, the branches creaked and groaned overhead, drops of rain pattered upon the leaves, mutterings of thunder were heard, and a lurid flash of lightning quivered down the gloomy avenue.

'I towd tha haa it ud be,' said Adam, and Robin simply answered--

'I'm no worse off than befooar. Let's mak' toart whoam; bud say nowt to aar fowk--it ud nobbut freeten th' wimmin.'

Before the two men reached the lodge gates a terrible storm burst over them, and through it they made their way to the distant village.

A great change came over Robin, and from being the foremost in every countryside marlock he became serious and reserved, invariably at the close of the day's work rambling away, as though anxious to shun mankind, or else spending the evening at Adam's talking over 'th' warnin'.' Strange to say, about a month afterwards he fell from a stack, and after lingering some time, during which he often deliriously rambled about the events of the dreadful night, he dozed away, Old Jemmy, the sexton, had another grave to open, and the grey-headed Adam was one of the bearers who carried Robin's corpse along the avenue in which they had so short a time before seen the fairy funeral.{10}

THE CHIVALROUS DEVIL.

About half-a-century ago there lived, in a lane leading away from a little village near Garstang, a poor idiot named Gregory. He was at once the sport and the terror of the young folks. Uniformly kind to them, carefully convoying them to the spots where, in his lonely rambles, he had noticed birds' nests, or pressing upon them the wild flowers he had gathered in the neighbouring woods and thickets, he received at their ungrateful hands all kinds of ill treatment, not always stopping short of personal violence. In this respect, however, the thoughtless children only followed the example set them by their elders, for seldom did poor Gregory pass along the row of cottages, dignified by the name of street, which constituted the village, without an unhandsome head being projected from the blacksmith's or cobbler's shop, or from a doorway, and a cruel taunt being sent after the idiot, who, in his ragged clothing, with his handful of harebells and primroses, and a wreath of green leaves round his battered, old hat, jogged along towards his mother's cottage, singing as he went, in a pathetic monotone, a snatch of an old Lancashire ballad.

In accordance with that holy law which, under such circumstances, influences woman's heart, the mother loved this demented lad with passionate fondness, all the tenderness with which her nature had been endowed having been called forth by the needs of the afflicted child, whose only haven of refuge from the harshness of his surroundings and the cruelty of those who, had not they been as ignorant as the hogs they fed, would have pitied and protected him, was her breast. Lavishing all her affection upon the poor lad, she had no kindness to spare for those who tormented him; and abstaining from any of those melodramatic and vulgar curses with which a person of less education would have followed those who abused her child, she studiously held herself aloof from her neighbours, and avoided meeting them, except when she was compelled to purchase food or other articles for her little household. This conduct gave an excuse for much ill feeling, and as the woman had no need to toil for her daily bread, and as her cottage was the neatest in the district, there was much jealousy.

One night, at a jovial gathering, it was arranged that a practical joke, of what was considered a very humorous kind, should be played upon the idiot. The boors selected one of their party, whose task it should be to attire himself in a white sheet, and to emerge into the lane when the poor lad should make his appearance. In accordance with this plan the pack of hobbledehoys watched the cottage night after night, in the hope of seeing the idiot leave the dwelling, and at length their patience was rewarded. They immediately hid themselves in the ditch, while the mock ghost concealed himself behind the trunk of a tree. The lad, not suspecting any evil, came along, humming, in his melancholy monotone, the usual fragment, and just before he reached the tree the sheeted figure slowly stepped forth to the accompaniment of the groanings and bellowings of his associates. They had expected to see the idiot flee in terror; but instead of so doing, he laughed loudly at the white figure, and then suddenly, as the expression of his face changed to one of intense interest, he shouted, 'Oh, oh! a black one! a black one!' Sure enough, a dark and terrible figure stood in the middle of the road. The mock ghost fled, with his companions at his heels, the real spectre chasing them hotly, and the idiot bringing up the rear, shouting at the top of his voice, 'Run, black devil! catch white devil!'

They were not long in reaching the village, down the street of which they ran faster than they ever had run before. Several of them darted into the smithy, where the blacksmith was scattering the sparks right and left as he hammered away at the witch-resisting horseshoes, and others fled into the inn, where they startled the gathered company of idle gossips; but the mock ghost kept on wildly, looking neither to the left nor to the right. The idiot had kept close behind the phantom at the heels of the mock ghost, and when at the end of the village the spectre vanished as suddenly as it had appeared, the lad ran a little faster and took its place. Of this, however, the white-sheeted young fellow was not aware, and, fearing every moment that the shadow would catch him in its awful embrace, he dashed down a by lane. Before he got very far, however, the idiot, who had gradually been lessening the distance between them, overtook and seized him by the neck. With a terrible cry the rustic fell headlong into the ditch, dragging Gregory with him as he fell. The latter was soon upon his feet, and dancing about the lane as he cried, 'Catch white devil! catch white devil!' The mock ghost, however, lay quiet enough among the nettles.

Roused by the story told by the affrighted ones who had rushed so unceremoniously into their presence, as well as by the startling cry of 'Run, black devil! catch white devil!' which the idiot had shouted as he sped past the door, several of the topers emerged from their abiding place; and as nothing could be seen of either mock ghost, spectre, or idiot, they bravely determined to go in search of them. As they passed along the road from the village, their attention was attracted by the cries which seemed to come from the lonely lane, and somewhat nervously making their way along it, they soon saw the idiot dancing about the side of the ditch. With a sudden access of courage, due to the presence of anything human, however weak, they hurried along, and as they drew nearer, the idiot paused in his gambols, and pointed to the mock ghost, who lay stretched in the shadow of the hedgerow. He was soon carried away to the village, where he lay ill for weeks.

The kindness of Gregory's mother to the sick lad's parents, who were very poor and could ill afford to provide the necessary comforts his condition required, caused public feeling to turn in her favour, and those who formerly had been loudest in defaming her became her warmest eulogists. Between the idiot and the young fellow, too, a strange friendship sprang up, and the pair might often be seen passing along the lanes, the idiot chanting his melancholy fragments to the companion whose cap he had adorned with wreaths of wild flowers.

With such a protector the idiot was quite safe, and, indeed, had the village children been wishful to torment Gregory, if the presence of this companion had not sufficed to restrain them, they had only to remember that it was in defence of poor Gregory the Evil One himself had raced through the village.{11}

THE ENCHANTED FISHERMAN.

There are few views in the north of England more beautiful than that which is seen from Morecambe, as the spectator looks over the beautiful bay, with its crescent coast-line of nearly fifty miles in extent. At low water the dazzling sands, streaked by silvery deceptive channels, stretch to the distant glimmering sea, the music of whose heavings comes but faintly on the gentle breeze; but at tide-time a magnificent expanse of rolling waves sweeps away to Peel, and is dotted over with red-sailed fishing boats and coasters. Far to the north the huge heather-covered Furness Fells stand sentinel-like over the waters, and above them, dimly seen through the faint blue haze, tower the grand mountains of the magic lake country. The scene is full of a sweet dream-like beauty; but there are times when the beautiful is swallowed in the majestic, as the mists come creeping over the sea, obscuring the coasts, and hiding everything save the white caps of the waves gleaming in the darkness, through which the muttering diapasons of the wind, as though in deep distress, sound mysteriously; or when, in winter, the moon is hidden by scudding clouds, and the huge rollers, driven before the breeze, dash themselves to death, as upon the blast come the solemn boom of a signal gun, and the faint cries of those in danger on the deep.

Years ago, however, before the little village of Poulton changed its name, and began to dream of becoming a watering-place, with terraces and hotels, instead of the picturesque, tumble-down huts of the fishermen, against which, from time immemorial, the spray had been dashed by the salt breezes, the only people who gazed upon the lovely prospect were, with the exception of an occasional traveller, the families of the toilers of the sea, and the rough-looking men themselves. These hardy fellows, accustomed to a wild life, and whose days from childhood had been spent on or by the sea, loved the deep with as much tenderness as a strong man feels towards a weak and wayward maiden, for they were familiar with its every mood, with the soothing wash of its wavelets when the sunbeams kissed the foam-bells, as they died on the white sands, and with the noise of the thunder of the breakers chased up the beach by the roaring gales.

One evening a number of these men were seated in the cosy kitchen of the John-o'-Gaunt, listening to 'Owd England' as he narrated some of his strange experiences.

'I moind,' said he, 'when I was nobbut a bit of a lad, Tum Grisdale
bein' dreawnt; an' now as we're tawkin' abeaut th' dangers o' th'
sonds, yo'll mebbi hearken to th' tale. Poor Tum was th' best cockler i'
Hest Bank, an' as ust to th' sands as a choilt is to th' face o' its mother;
but for o that he wir dreawnt on 'em after o. I can co to moind yet--
for young as I wor I're owd enough to think a bit when owt quare
happent, an' th' seet o' th' deead bodies th' next ebb wir wi' me day
an' neet fur lung afterwart--th' day when Tum an' his missis an' th' two
lasses seet eawt o' seein' some relations o' th' missis's soide, as livt i' th'
Furness country yon, th' owd mon an' th' dowters i' th' shandray, an'
th' missis ridin' upo' th' cowt at th' soide. It wir a gradely bonnie
afternoon, at th' back eend o' th' year. Th' day as they should o
come back wir varra misty; an' abaat th' edge o' dark, just as here
an' theear a leet wir beginnin' to twinkle i' th' windows, an' th' stars to
peep aat, th' noise ov a cart comin' crunchin' o'er th' beach tuk mi
feyther to th' door. "Why, yon's owd Tum Grisdale cart back
ageean," he cried eaut. An' he dartit eawt o' th' dur, an' me after, as
fast as I could. A creawd o' folk an' childer soon gathert reawnt,
wonderin' what wir up; but neawt could bi larnt, for though th' lasses
as seet eawt, as breet an' bonnie as posies o gillivers, wir theear i' th'
shandray, they wir too freetent an' dazed, an' too wake wi' th' weet
an' cowd, to say a whord. One thing, however, wir sewer enough,
th' owd folk hedn't come back; an' altho' th' toide then hed covert
th' track, an' wir shinin' i' th' moonleet, wheear th' mist could bi sin
through, just as if it hedn't mony a Hest Bank mon's life to answer for,
a lot o' young cocklers wir for startin' off theear an' then i' search on
'em. Th' owder an' mooar expayrienced, heawiver, wodn't hear on
it. Two lives i' one day wir quoite enough, they said; so they o waitit
till th' ebb, an' then startit, me, loile as i'wir, among th' rest, for mi
feyther wir too tekken up i' talking to send me whoam. It wir a sad
outin', but it wir loively compaart wi' t' comin' back, for when we
tornt toart Hest Bank, th' strungest o' th' lads carriet owd Tum an' his
missis, for we hedn't getten far o'er th' sonds afooar we feawnt th'
poor owd lass, an' not far off, i' th' deep channel, owd Tum hissel.
They wir buriet i' th' owd church-yart, an' one o' th' lasses wir laid
aside on 'em, th' freet hevin' bin too mich for her. When t' tother sister
recovert a bit, an' could bide to talk abaat it, hoo said as they geet
lost i' th' mist, an' th' owd mon left 'em i' th' shandray while he walkt a
bit to foind th' channel. When he didn't come back they geet
freetent, but t' owd woman wodn't stir fray th' spot till they heeart t'
watters comin', an' then they went a bit fur, but could find nowt o'
Tum, though they thowt neaw an' then they could heear him

sheautin' to 'em. Th' sheawts, heawiver, geet fainter an' fainter, an'
at last stopt o' together. Givin' thersels up for lost, they left th' reins to
th' mare an' t' cowt. Th' poor owd lass wir quoite daz't at th' absence
o' Tum; an' as th' cowt wir swimmin' across th' channel hoo lost her
howd, an' wir carriet away. Th' lasses knew neawt no mooar, th'
wench olus said, till th' fowk run deawn to th' cart uppo' th' beach.
Hor as wir left, hoo wir olus quare at after; an' hoo uset to walk alung
t' bay at o heawers just at th' toide toime, yo' known, an' it wir pitiful
t' heear her when th' woint wir a bit sriller nor usal, sayin' as hoo could
heear her owd fayther's voice as he sheauted when hee'd wander't
fray 'em an' couldn't foint way to 'em through t' mist. Hoo afterwarts
went to sarvice at Lankister, to a place as th' paason fun' for her, i'
th' idea o' th' change dooin' her good; but it worn't lung afooar th'
news come as hoo wir i' th' 'sylum, an' I heeart as hoo deed theear
some toime after.'

No sooner had the grey-headed old fisherman finished his story than
one of the auditors said, 'Hoo met weel fancy hoo heeart th' voice
ov her fayther, for monnie a neet, an' monnie another hev I heeart
that cry mysen. Yo' may stare, bud theear's mooar saands to be
heeard i' th' bay nor some o' yo' lads known on; an' I'm no choilt to
be freetent o' bein' i' th' dark. Why nobbut th' neet afooar last I
heeart a peal o' bells ringin' under th' watter.'{12} There was a
moment of surprise, for Roger Heathcote was not a likely man to be
a victim to his own fancies, or to be influenced by the superstitions
which clung to his fellows. Like the rest of his companions, he had
spent the greatest portion of his life away from land; and either
because he possessed keener powers of observation than they, or
loved nature more, and therefore watched her more closely, he
had gradually added to his store of knowledge, until he had
become the recognised authority on all matters connected with the
dangerous calling by which the men-folk of the little colony earned
daily bread for their families. As he was by no means addicted to
yarns, looks of wonder came over the faces of the listeners; and in
deference to the wishes of Old England, who pressed him as to what
he had heard and seen, Roger narrated the adventure embodied in
this story.{13}

* * * * *

The fisherman's little boat was dancing lightly on the rippling waters
of the bay.

The night was perfectly calm, the moon shining faintly through a thin mist which rested on the face of the deep. It was nearly midnight, and Roger was thinking of making for home, when he heard the sweet sounds of a peal of bells. Not without astonishment, he endeavoured to ascertain from what quarter the noises came, and, strange and unlikely as it seemed, it appeared that the chimes rang up through the water, upon which, with dreamy motion, his boat was gliding. Bending over the side of the skiff he again heard with singular distinctness the music of the bells pealing in weird beauty. For some time he remained in this attitude, intently listening to the magical music, and when he arose, the mist had cleared off, and the moon was throwing her lovely light upon the waters, and over the distant fells. Instead, however, of beholding a coast with every inch of which he was acquainted, Roger gazed upon a district of which he knew nothing. There were mountains, but they were not those whose rugged outlines were so vividly impressed upon his memory. There was a beach, but it was not the one where his little cottage stood with its light in the window and its background of wind-bent trees. The estuary into which his boat was gliding was not that of the Kent, with its ash and oak-covered crags. Everything seemed unreal, even the streaming moonlight having an unusual whiteness, and Roger rapidly hoisted his little sails, but they only flapped idly against the mast, as the boat, in obedience to an invisible and unknown agency, drifted along the mysterious looking river. As the fisherman gazed in helpless wonder, gradually the water narrowed, and in a short time a cove was gained, the boat grating upon the gleaming sand. Roger at once jumped upon the bank, and no sooner had he done so, than a number of little figures clad in green ran towards him from beneath a clump of trees, the foremost of them singing--To the home of elf and fay, To the land of nodding flowers,To the land of Ever Day Where all things own the Fay Queen's powers,

Mortal come away!

and the remainder dancing in circles on the grass, and joining in the refrain--To the home of elf and fay,To the land of Ever Day,

Mortal come away!

The song finished, the little fellow who had taken the solo, tripped daintily to Roger, and, with a mock bow, grasped one of the fingers of the fisherman's hand, and stepped away as though anxious to lead him from the water.

Assuming that he had come upon a colony of Greenies, and feeling assured that such tiny beings could not injure him, even if anxious to do so, Roger walked on with his conductor, the band dancing in a progressing circle in front of them, until a wood was reached, when the dancers broke up the ring and advanced in single file between the trees. The light grew more and more dim, and when the cavalcade reached the entrance to a cavern, Roger could hardly discern the Greenies. Clinging to the little hand of his guide, however, the undaunted fisherman entered the cave, and groped his way down a flight of mossy steps. Suddenly he found himself in a beautiful glade, in which hundreds of little figures closely resembling his escort, and wearing dainty red caps, were disporting themselves and singing--Moonbeams kissing odorous bowersLight our home amid the flowers;While our beauteous King and QueenWatch us dance on rings of green. Rings of green, rings of green, Dance, dance, dance, on rings of green.

No sooner had the fisherman entered the glade than the whole party crowded round him, but as they did so a strain of enchanting music was heard, and the little beings hopped away again, and whirled round in a fantastic waltz. Roger himself was so powerfully influenced by the melody that he flung himself into the midst of the dancers, who welcomed him with musical cries, and he capered about until sheer fatigue forced him to sink to rest upon a flowery bank. Here, after watching for a while the graceful gambols of the Greenies, and soothed by the weird music, the sensuous odours, and the dreamy light, he fell into a deep sleep. When he awoke from his slumber the fairies had vanished, and the fisherman felt very hungry. No sooner, however, had he wished for something to eat than on the ground before him there appeared a goodly array of delicacies, of which, without more ado, Roger partook.

'I'm in luck's way here,' he said to himself; 'It's not every day of the week I see a full table like this. I should like to know where I am, though.' As the wish passed his lips he saw before him a beautiful little being, who said in a sweet low voice--In the land of nodding flowers,Where all things own the Fay Queen's powers!

The fisherman no sooner saw the exquisite face of the dainty Greenie than he forgot altogether the rosy-cheeked wife at home, and fell hopelessly over head and ears in love with the sweet vision.

Gazing into her beautiful eyes he blurted out, 'I don't care where it is if you are there.' With a smile the queen, for it was indeed the queen, seated herself at his side. 'Dost thou, Mortal, bow to my power?' asked she. 'Ay, indeed, do I to the forgetfulness of everything but thy bonny face,' answered Roger; upon which the queen burst into a hearty fit of laughter, so musical, however, that for the life of him the fisherman could not feel angry with her. 'If the king were to hear thee talking thus thou wouldst pay dearly for thy presumption,' said the Fay, as she rose and tripped away to the shadow of the trees. The enraptured Roger endeavoured to overtake her before she reached the oaks, but without success; and though he wandered through the wood for hours, he did not again catch a glimpse of her. He gained an appetite by the freak however, and no sooner had he wished for food again than dishes of rich viands appeared before him.

'I wish I could get money at this rate,' said the fisherman, and the words had hardly left his lips when piles of gold ranged themselves within his reach. Roger rapidly filled his pockets with the glittering coins, and even took the shoes from off his feet, and filled them also, and then slung them round his neck by the strings.

'Now, if I could but get to my boat,' thought he, 'my fortune would be made,' and accordingly he began to make his way in what he believed to be the direction of the river. He had not proceeded very far, however, when he emerged upon an open space surrounded by tall foxgloves,{14} in all the beautiful bells of which dreamy-eyed little beings were swinging lazily as the quiet zephyr rocked their perfumed dwellings. Some of the Greenies were quite baby fairies not so large as Roger's hand, but none of them seemed alarmed at the presence of a mortal. A score of larger ones were hard at work upon the sward stitching together moth and butterfly wings for a cloak for their Queen, who, seated upon a mushroom, was smiling approvingly as she witnessed the industry of her subjects. Roger felt a sudden pang as he observed her, for although he was glad once more to behold the marvellous beauty of her face, he was jealous of a dainty dwarf in a burnished suit of beetles' wing cases and with a fantastic peaked cap in which a red feather was coquettishly stuck, for this personage he suspected was the King, and forgetting his desire to escape with the gold, and at once yielding to his feelings, he flung himself on the luxuriant grass near the little being whose weird loveliness had thrown so strange a glamour over him, and without any thought or fear as to the consequences he at once bent himself and kissed one of her dainty sandalled feet. No sooner had he performed this rash act of devotion than numberless blows fell upon him from all sides, but he was unable to see any of the beings by whom he was struck. Instinctively the fisherman flung his huge fists about wildly, but without hitting any of the invisible Greenies, whose tantalising blows continued to fall upon him. At length, however, wearying of the fruitless contest, he roared out, 'I wish I were safe in my boat in the bay,' and almost instantaneously he found himself in the little skiff, which was stranded high and dry upon the Poulton beach. The shoes which he had so recently filled with glittering pieces of gold and suspended round his neck were again upon his feet, his pockets were as empty as they were when he had put out to sea some hours before, and somewhat dubious and very disgusted, in a few minutes he had crept off to bed.

* * * * *

When the strange tale of the fisherman's wonderful adventure with the hill folk was ended, the unbelievers did not hesitate to insinuate that Roger had not been out in the bay at all, and that the land of nodding flowers might be found by anyone who stayed as long and chalked up as large a score at the John-o'-Gaunt as he had done on the night when he heard the submerged bells and had so unusual a catch.

Others, however, being less sceptical, many were the little boats that afterwards went on unsuccessful voyages in search of the mysterious estuary and the colony of Greenies, and a year afterwards, when a sudden gale swept over the restless face of the deep and cast Roger's boat bottom upwards upon the sandy beach, many believed that the fisherman had again found the land of Ever Day.

THE SANDS OF COCKER.

The quiet little village of Cockerham is hardly the spot one would expect to find selected as a place of residence by a gentleman of decidedly fast habits, and to whom a latch-key is indispensable; yet once upon a time the Evil One himself, it is said, took up his quarters in the go-to-bed-early hamlet. It hardly need be stated that the undesirable resident caused no small stir in the hitherto drowsy little place. Night after night he prowled about with clanking chains, and shed an unpleasantly-suggestive odour of sulphur, that rose to the diamond-paned windows and crept through cracks and chinks to the nasal organs of the horrified villagers, who had been disturbed by the ringing of the Satanic bracelets, and, fearing to sleep whilst there was so strong a smell of brimstone about, lay awake, thinking of the sins they had committed, or intended to commit if they escaped 'Old Skrat.'

Before the wandering perfumer had thus, above a score of times, gratuitously fumigated the villagers, a number of the more daring ones, whose courage rose when they found that after all they were not flown away with, resolved that they would have a meeting, at which the unjustifiable conduct of a certain individual should be discussed, and means be devised of ridding the village of his odoriferous presence. In accordance with this determination, a gathering was announced for noonday, for the promoters of the movement did not dare to assemble after sunset to discuss such a subject. After a few cursory remarks from the chairman, and a long and desultory discussion as to the best way of getting rid of the self-appointed night watchman, it was settled that the schoolmaster, as the most learned man in the place, should be the deputation, and have all the honour and profit of an interview with the nocturnal rambler.

Strange as it may appear, the pedagogue was nothing loath to accept the office, for if there was one thing more than another for which he had longed, it was an opportunity of immortalising himself; the daily round of life in the village certainly affording but few chances of winning deathless fame. He therefore at once agreed to take all the risks if he might also have all the glory. Not that he purposed to go to the Devil; no, the mountain should come to Mahomet; the Evil One should have the trouble of coming to him.

His determination was loudly applauded by the assembled villagers, each of whom congratulated himself upon an escape from the dangerous, if noble, task of ridding the place of an intolerable nuisance.

There was no time to be lost, and a night or two afterwards, no sooner had the clock struck twelve, than the schoolmaster, who held a branch of ash and a bunch of vervain in his hand, chalked the conventional circle{15} upon the floor of his dwelling, stepped within it, and in a trembling voice began to repeat the Lord's Prayer backwards. When he had muttered about half of the spell thunder began to roar in the distance; rain splashed on the roof, and ran in streams from the eaves; a gust of wind moaned round the house, rattling the loose leaded panes, shaking the doors, and scattering the embers upon the hearth. At the same time the solitary light, which had begun to burn a pale and ghastly blue, was suddenly extinguished, as though by an invisible hand; but the terrified schoolmaster was not long left in darkness, for a vivid flash of lightning illuminated the little chamber, and almost blinded the would-be necromancer, who tried to gabble a prayer in the orthodox manner, but his tongue refused to perform its office, and clave to the roof of his mouth.

At that moment, could he have made his escape, he would willingly have given to the first comer all the glory he had panted to achieve; but even had he dared to leave the magic circle, there was not time to do so, for almost immediately there was a second blast of wind, before which the trees bent like blades of grass, a second flash lighted up the room, a terrible crash of thunder shook the house to its foundations, and, as a number of evil birds, uttering doleful cries, dashed themselves through the window, the door burst open, and the schoolmaster felt that he was no longer alone.

An instantaneous silence, dreadful by reason of the contrast, followed, and the moon peeped out between the driving clouds and threw its light into the chamber. The birds perched themselves upon the window sill and ceased to cry, and with fiery-looking eyes peered into the room, and suddenly the trembling amateur saw the face of the dark gentleman whose presence only a few minutes before he had so eagerly desired.

Overpowered by the sight, his knees refused to bear him up, what little hair had not been removed from his head by the stupidity of the rising generation stood on end, and with a miserable groan he sank upon his hands and knees, but, fortunately for himself, within the magic ring, round which the Evil One was running rapidly. How long this gratuitous gymnastic entertainment continued he knew not, for he was not in a state of mind to judge of the duration of time, but it seemed an age to the unwilling observer, who, afraid of having the Devil behind him, and yielding to a mysterious mesmeric influence, endeavoured, by crawling round backward, to keep the enemy's face in front. At length, however, the saltatory fiend asked in a shrill and unpleasant voice,

'Rash fool, what wantest thou with me? Couldst thou not wait until in the ultimate and proper course of things we had met?'

Terrified beyond measure not only at the nature of the pertinent question, but also by the insinuation and the piercing and horrible tone in which it was spoken, the tenant of the circle knew not what reply to make, and merely stammered and stuttered--

'Good Old Nick,{16} go away for ever, and'--

'Take thee with me,' interrupted the Satanic one quickly. 'Even so; such is my intent.'

Upon this the poor wretch cried aloud in terror, and again the Evil One began to hop round and round and round the ring, evidently in the hope of catching a part of the body of the occupant projecting over the chalk mark.

'Is there no escape,' plaintively asked the victim in his extremity, 'is there no escape?'

Upon this Old Nick suddenly stopped his gambols and quietly said,

'Three chances of escape shalt thou have,{17} but if thou failest, then there is no appeal. Set me three tasks, and if I cannot perform any one of them, then art thou free.'

There was a glimmer of hope in this, and the shivering necromancer brightened up a little, actually rising from his ignoble position and once more standing erect, as he gleefully said,

'I agree.'

'Ah, ah,' said the Evil One _sotto voce_.

'Count the raindrops on the hedgerows from here to Ellel,' cried the schoolmaster.

'Thirteen,' immediately answered Satan, 'the wind I raised when I came shook all the others off.'

'One chance gone,' said the wizard, whose knees again began to manifest signs of weakness.

There was a short pause, the schoolmaster evidently taking time to consider, for, after all, life, even in a place like Cockerham, was sweet in comparison with what might be expected in the society of the odoriferous one whose mirth was so decidedly ill-timed and unmusical. The silence was not of long continuance, however, for the Evil One began to fear that a detestably early cock might crow, and thereby rescue the trembling one from his clutches. In his impatience, therefore, he knocked upon the floor with his cloven hoof and whistled loudly, after the manner followed now-a-days by dirty little patrons of the drama, perched high in the gallery of a twopenny theatre, and again danced rapidly round the ring in what the tenant deemed unnecessary proximity to the chalk mark.

'Count the ears of corn in old Tithepig's field,' suddenly cried the schoolmaster.

'Three millions and twenty-six,' at once answered Satan.

'I have no way of checking it,' moaned the pedagogue.

'Ah, ah,' bellowed the fiend, who now, instead of hopping round the ring, capered in high glee about the chamber.

'Ho, ho!' laughed the schoolmaster, 'I have it! Here it is! Ho, ho! Twist a rope of sand{18} and wash it in the river Cocker without losing a grain.'

The Evil One stepped out of the house, to the great relief of its occupier, who at once felt that the atmosphere was purer; but in a few minutes he returned with the required rope of sand.

'Come along,' said he, 'and see it washed.' And he swung it over his shoulder, and stepped into the lane.

In the excitement of the moment the wizard had almost involuntarily stepped out of the magic circle, when suddenly he bethought himself of the danger, and drily said--

'Thank you; I'll wait here. By the light of the moon I can see you wash it.'

The baffled fiend, without more ado, stepped across to the rippling streamlet, and dipped the rope into the water, but when he drew it out he gave utterance to a shout of rage and disappointment, for half of it had been washed away.

'Hurrah!' shouted the schoolmaster. 'Cockerham against the world!' And as in his joy he jumped out of the ring, the Evil One, instead of seizing him, in one stride crossed Pilling Moss and Broadfleet, and vanished, and from that night to the present day Cockerham has been quite free from Satanic visits.{19}

THE SILVER TOKEN.

Believe i' Fairies? 'Ay, that I do, though I never clapped mi een on 'em,' said old Nancy to a group of gaping listeners seated by the farm-house kitchen fire.

'That's quare,' remarked a sceptical young woman in the ingle nook.

Old Nancy gave her a scornful glance, and then went on:--

'I never see'd a fairy as I know on, but I used to sarve one on 'em wi' milk. Yo' mon stare; but th' way on it wir this. I wir at mi wark i' th' dairy one day, abaat th' edge o' dark, when o ov a suddent a loile jug clapt itsel daan afooar mi on th' stooan. Yo' may be sure I wir fair capt, for wheear it come fray, or heaw it geet theear, I couldn't mek aat. I stoopt mi daan to pike howd on it, and it met a' bin silver, it wir that breet and bonnie; but it wir as leet as a feather, an' I couldn't tell what it wir med on. I wir baan to set it o' th' stooan again, when I seed at a new sixpenny bit hed bin put theer wi' it, so it struck mi as milk wir wantit. Accordingly I fillt th' jug and seet it daan again, an' welly as soon as I'd clapt it wheear I fun' it, it up an' whipt eaut o' seet. Well I thowt it meeterly quare, bud I'd heeard mi feyther say, monny an' monny a toime, as thuse as geet fairy brass gin 'em should tell nubry, so I kept it to mysen, though I'd hard wark, yo' may be sure. Every neet th' jug an' th' sixpenny bit clapt theirsens o' th' stooan as reglar as milkin' toime, an' I fillt th' jug and piked up th' brass. At last, ha'ever, I thowt happen no lumber could come on it if I towd nobbut one, so when Roger theear and me settlet a beein wed I towd him what sooart ov a nest-egg I'd getten so quarely. Mi feyther wir reet, ha'ever, for th' next neet nayther jug nor th' sixpenny bit showed thersels, an' fray that day to this I've sin no mooar on 'em, an' it's ower forty year sin I piked up th' last brass.{3}</p>

THE HEADLESS WOMAN.
(BEAWT HEEOD.)

It was near upon twelve when Gabriel Fisher bade good night to the
assembled roysterers who were singing and shouting in the kitchen
of the White Bull, at Longridge, and, turning his back to the cosy
hearth, upon which a huge log was burning, emerged into the
moonlit road. With his dog Trotty close at his heels, he struck out
manfully towards Tootal Height and Thornley, for he had a long and
lonely walk before him. It was a clear and frosty night, but
occasionally a light cloud sailed across the heavens, and obscured
the moon. Rapidly passing between the two rows of cottages which
constituted the little straggling village, his footsteps ringing upon the
frozen ground, Gabriel made for the fells, and, as he hurried along,
he hummed to himself a line of the last song he had heard, and now
and again burst into a fit of laughter as he remembered a humorous
story told by 'Owd Shuffler.' When he reached the highest point of
the road whence he could see the beautiful Chipping valley, a soft
breeze was whispering among the fir-trees, with that faint rustle
suggestive of the gentle fall of waves upon a beach. Here and there
a little white farm-house or labourer's cottage was gleaming in the
moonlight, but the inmates had been asleep for hours. There was an
air of loneliness and mystery over everything; and though Gabriel
would have scorned to admit that he was afraid of anything living or
dead, before he had passed out of the shadow of the weird-looking
melodious branches he found himself wishing for other company
than that of his dog. He suddenly remembered, too, with no access
of pleasurable feelings, that on the previous day he had seen a
solitary magpie, and all sorts of stories of 'Banister Dolls' and 'Jinny
Greenteeths,' with which his youthful soul had been carefully
harrowed, came across his mind. He tried to laugh at these
recollections, but the attempt was by no means a successful one,
and he gave expression to a hearty wish that Kemple End were not
quite so far off.

Just then a sharp shrill cry fell upon his ear, and then another and
another. 'Th' Gabriel Ratchets,'{33} he shouted, 'what's abaat to
happen?' The cries were not repeated, however, and he went on,
but when he reached the peak of the fell, and gazed before him
into the deep shade of a plantation, he could not repress a slight
shudder, for he fancied that he saw something moving at a
distance. He paused for a moment or two to assure himself, and
then went on again slowly, his heart throbbing violently as he

---

lessened the space between the moving object and himself. The dog, as though equally influenced by similar feelings, crept behind him in a suspicious and terrified manner.

'It's nobbut a woman,' said he, somewhat re-assured; 'it's a woman sewerly. Mebbee someburry's badly, an' hoo's gooin' for help. Come on, Trotty, mon.'

So saying, he quickened his pace, the dog hanging behind, until he approached almost close to the figure, when, with a wild howl, away Trotty fled down the hillside. As Gabriel drew still closer, he saw that the object wore a long light cloak and hood, and a large coal-scuttle bonnet; and surprised to find that the sound of his footsteps did not cause her to turn to see who was following, he called out:

'It's a bonny neet, Missis; bud yo're aat rayther late, arn't yo'?'

'It is very fine,' answered the woman, in a voice which Gabriel thought was the sweetest he had ever heard, but without turning towards him as she spoke.

'Summat wrong at your fowk's, happen?' he asked, anxious to prolong the talk. There was no reply to this, though, and Gabriel knew not what to think, for the silent dame, although she declined to reply, continued to keep pace with him, and to walk at his side. Was it some one who had no business to be out at that hour, and who did not wish to be recognised, he wondered? But if so, thought he, why did she continue to march in a line with him? The voice, certainly, was that of one of a different rank to his own; but, on the other hand, he reflected, if she were one of the gentle folks, why the cottager's cloak and bonnet, and the huge market basket? These conjectures crossed his brain in rapid succession; and influenced by the last one--that as to his companion's clothing--he determined again to address her.

'Yo' met a left yir tung at whoam, Missis,' said he, 'sin' yo' connot answer a civil mon.'

This taunt, however, like the direct query, failed to provoke an answer, although the startled Gabriel could have sworn that a smothered laugh came from beneath the white cloth which covered the contents of the basket 'Let me carry yer baskit,' said he; 'it's heavy for yo'.'

Without a word, the woman held it out to him; but, as Gabriel grasped the handle, a voice, which sounded as though the mouth of the speaker were close to his hand, slowly said:

'You're very kind, I'm sure;' and then there came from the same quarter a silvery peal of laughter.

'What i' th' warld can it be?' said Gabriel, as without more ado he let the basket fall to the ground. He did not remain in ignorance very long, however, for, as the white cloth slipped off, a human head, with fixed eyes, rolled out 'Th' yedless boggart!' cried he, as the figure turned to pick up the head, and revealed to him an empty bonnet, and away he fled down the hill, fear lending him speed. He had not run far, however, before he heard a clatter of feet on the hard road behind him; but Gabriel was one of the fleetest lads about the fells, and the sight he had just seen was calculated to bring out all his powers; so the sound did not grow louder, but just as he turned into the old Chaighley Road, the head, thrown by the boggart, came whizzing past in unpleasant proximity to his own, and went rolling along in front of him. For a second or two Gabriel hesitated what to do, the headless woman behind and the equally terrible head in front; but it did not take long to decide, and he went forward with renewed vigour, thinking to pass the dreadful thing rapidly rolling along in advance of him. No sooner was he near to it, however, than, with an impish laugh, which rang in his ears for days afterwards, the ghastly object diverged from its course and rolled in his way. With a sudden and instinctive bound, he leaped over it; and as he did so the head jumped from the ground and snapped at his feet, the teeth striking together with a dreadfully suggestive clash. Gabriel was too quick for it, however, but for some distance he heard with horrible distinctness the clattering of the woman's feet and the banging of the head upon the road behind him.

Gradually the sounds grew fainter as he speeded along, and at length, after he had crossed a little stream of water which trickled across the lane from a fern-covered spring in the fell side, the sounds ceased altogether. The runner, however, did not pause to take breath until he had reached his home and had crept beneath the blankets, the trembling Trotty, whom he found crouched in terror at the door of the cottage, skulking upstairs at his heels and taking refuge under the bed.

'I olus said as tha'd be seein' a feeorin wi' thi stoppin' aat o' neets,' remarked his spouse after he had narrated his adventure; 'bud if it nobbut meks tha fain o' thi own haath-stooan I'se be some glad on it, for it's moor nor a woman wi' a heead on her shoothers hes bin able to do.'{20}

THE RESCUE OF MOONBEAM.

From one corner of Ribbleton Moor, the scene of Cromwell's victory over Langdale, there is as lovely a view as ever painter dreamed of. Far below the spectator the Ribble sweeps almost in a circle beneath the scars which, by the action of years of this washing, have been scooped out so as to form a large precipice, under which the waters flow, marking out in their course the great 'horse-shoe meadow,' with its fringe of shining sand. The peaceful valley through which the river, reflecting in its moving bosom the overhanging many-tinted woods and cliffs, meanders on its way to the sea, is bounded afar-off by noble hills, the whale-like Pendle towering in majestic grandeur above the rest. From the moor a rough and stony lane winds down the wooded hillside, past a beautiful old half-timbered house down to the dusty highway and the bridge over the Belisamia of the Romans. The beautiful river, with its tremulous earth and sky pictures, the meadows and corn-fields whence come now and again the laugh and song of the red-faced mowers and reapers, the clearly-defined roads and white farm-houses, the spires of distant hillside churches, and the rich green of the waving woods, make up an enchanting picture. When night comes, however, and the lovely stars peep out, and the crescent moon casts her glamour over the dreaming earth, and half-hidden in a dimly transparent veil of shimmering mist the Ribble glides as gently as though it had paused to listen to its own melody, a still deeper loveliness falls upon the dreaming landscape, over which the very genius of beauty seems to hover silently with outspread wings.

At such a time, when moon and stars threw a faint and mysterious light over the sleeping woods, and not a sound, save the cry of a restless bird, broke the silence, a young countryman made his way rapidly across the horse-shoe meadow to the bend of the stream under Red Scar.

It was not to admire the beautiful scenery, however, that Reuben Oswaldwistle was crossing the dew-besprinkled field, over which faint odours of hay were wafted by a gentle breeze. The sturdy young fellow was too practical to yield entirely to such an influence, and although he was by no means unlearned in the traditions and stories of the neighbourhood, long familiarity had taught him to look upon the landscape with the eye of a farmer. He was simply about to practise the gentle art in the hope of beguiling a few stray 'snigs' for dinner on the following day. Still the scene in all its glamour of moonlight and peace was not powerless even upon his rude nature; so, after setting his lines, he took out a little black pipe, filled it from a capacious moleskin pouch, and after lighting the fragrant weed, gave way to a train of disconnected fancies--past, present, and future mingling strangely in his reverie.

What with the rustling of the leaves overhead, the musical rippling of the river as it danced over the stones on its way to the sea, and the soothing effect of the tobacco, Reuben was beginning to doze, when suddenly he fancied he heard the sound of a light footstep in the grass behind him. Turning round somewhat drowsily, he beheld a little figure of about a span high, clad in green, and wearing a dainty red cap, struggling along under the load of a flat-topped mushroom much larger than itself. After having more than once fallen with its load, the dwarf cried out in a sweet, faint voice, 'Dewdrop, Dewdrop!' and no sooner had the sound died into silence than another little fellow, who evidently answered to the pretty name, came tripping from the shadow of a hawthorn.

'What's the matter, Moonbeam?' said the new-comer, cheerily.

'This table is too much for me,' answered the labourer whom Reuben had seen first, 'and if the king's dinner is not ready to a minute he will have me stung. Help me with this load, there's a good sort.'

Without any more ado Dewdrop came forward and the tiny pair put their shoulders beneath the load and marched off. They did not bear it very far, however, for the astonished Reuben simply stretched himself at full length on the grass and again was quite close to them.

The two dots stopped when they came to a hole, into which they at once stuck the stem of the mushroom. Moonbeam then took from his pocket a butterfly's wing, which served him as a handkerchief, and wiping his forehead as he spoke, he said:--

'I'm about tired of this. Every night the table is stolen, Dewdrop, and I've to find a new one for each dinner, and no thanks for it either. What has come of late over the king I am at a loss to imagine, for he has done nothing but have me stung. I shall emigrate if this continues, that's all.'

'So would I,' answered the other little fellow, 'if Blue-eyes would go also, but I can't leave her.'

After a hearty peal of laughter, during which he had held his shaking sides, Moonbeam shouted--

'Why, my dear innocent, if you went she would be after you in a trice. I remember that when I was as guileless as you I fell in love with Ravenhair, the daughter of old Pigear. She treated me just as Blue-eyes uses you, but when, in a fit of jealous rage, I began to pay delicate attentions to Jasmine, the tables soon were turned, and one evening, as I was dozing in a flower cup, I heard some one call me, and peeping out of my chamber, I saw the once scornful Ravenhair weeping at the foot of the stalk. No sooner did she catch a glimpse of the tip of my nightcap than in piteous tones, that went straight to my heart, she cried out, "Dearest Moony, let me come up and"--. But, hush! wasn't that the dinner gong?'

The pair listened intently as over the grass came the solemn hum of a bee.

'I'm in for it,' said the fairy whose tale had been so suddenly interrupted; 'there's the first bell, and I haven't got even the table set.'

The pair darted off, and tripping away into the shade of the hawthorn, they were for a moment or two lost to the sight of the wondering Reuben, but they soon returned, each bearing a dish and cover made of a little pearl shell. These they placed upon the mushroom, and away they scudded, again to return in a minute with another load. In an incredibly short space of time the table was set out with a goodly array of tiny dishes and plates.

Once more the hum of the bee was heard booming over the grass, and from the shadow of the tree there emerged a dainty being whose attire glittered in the moonlight, and whose step was like that of a proud monarch. He was clad in a many-hued coat made of wings of dragon flies, a green vest cut from a downy mouse-ear leaf, and with buttons of buttercup buds; little knee-breeches of fine-spun silk dyed in the juice of a whinberry, stockings of cobweb, and shoes of shining beetle case; his shirt, which was as white as falling snow, had been cut from convolvulus flowers ere they had opened to the light; and his hat, a gem of a thing fit only for a fairy, was of red poppy, with a waving white feather, and a band of fur from a

---

caterpillar. He led by the hand another personage, equally daintily dressed, but of a higher order of loveliness, with a pale oval face, and dreamy-looking eyes, gleaming like the sea when the moon and stars are bending over its bosom, and the wind is whispering its sad secrets. Her hair was golden, and rippled almost to her exquisite feet, and over it she wore a blue cornflower wreath, with diamond dewdrops here and there amid the leaves. Her dress was of damask rose leaves looped up with myosotis.

The grass hardly bent beneath her, so daintily did she trip along, just touching the tips of the fingers of the hand the king extended to her. Following this royal pair came a group of gaily-clad attendants, and a band discoursing sweet sounds, the deep bass of bees harmonising happily with the barytone of a beetle and the crescendo chirp of a cricket.

With a loud flourish from the musicians all took their places at the festive mushroom, and the banquet began. The dishes were sufficiently various to tempt even an anchorite to excess, for all the delicacies of the season were there. Ladybird soup, baked stickleback, roasted leg of nightingale, boiled shoulder of frog with cranberry sauce, wild strawberry tarts, and numerous kinds of fruits and juices, made up a dainty repast, of which king, queen, and courtiers partook heartily. The band, the members of which were perched in the swinging flowers of a foxglove close by, played lustily during the feast.

'For once,' said the king, 'for once--and let the circumstance be remembered when the annals of our reign are written--a day hath passed without anything having annoyed our royal self, without anything unpleasant having happened in our royal presence, and without anything having disagreed with our royal stomach.'

No sooner had these words passed the royal lips, however, than the queen gave a faint shriek, and cried out--

'My love, there is not a drop of my chickweed wine on the table.'

A dark cloud passed over the monarch's face as he angrily shouted--

'Methinks we were congratulating our royal self somewhat too early in the day. Bring hither the rascally Moonbeam and bid the executioners attend for orders.'

One of the courtiers, with an alacrity marvellously resembling that of beings of a larger growth, rushed out, and speedily returned with the unfortunate dependant, who at once flung himself on the ground before the angry king and begged to be forgiven. What result might have followed these prayers is uncertain, for, unfortunately, the suppliant's tears fell upon one of the monarch's shoes and dimmed its lustre.

'Bring hither the executioners and their instruments,' roared the infuriated king, and almost immediately a couple of sturdy little fellows appeared leading by a chain two large wasps.

'Do your disreputable work!' shouted the monarch.

The executioners seized Moonbeam, fastened him to a stake, and pressed a wasp against him. The insect instantly stung him, and the miserable little fellow howled with pain.

'Take him away,' cried the queen; 'we don't want _whine_ of that kind.'

'What a wretched pun!' involuntarily said Moonbeam, as they were dragging him from the royal presence.

'Bring the villain back,' roared the King; 'bring him back, and sting him until he is less critical.'

'If tha hez him stung ageeon,' interrupted the indignant Reuben, who in his excitement had gradually crept nearer to the royal table, 'I'll knock thi proud little heeod off, chuz who tha art.'

Neither the king or the executioners, however, took the slightest notice of the warning, so, as the latter were once more forcing the unhappy Moonbeam against the other wasp, down came a huge fist upon the royal head.

'Theer,' said the fisherman, exultingly, 'I towd tha, didn't I, bud tha wouldn't tek wernin'. Tha 'rt on 't' penitent form bi this time, I daat.'

Lifting up his hand, however, what was the surprise of the wondering Reuben to find only a little crushed grass under it. King, Queen,

---

courtiers, Moonbeam, executioners, and wasps, all had vanished, and even the band, whose humming and droning he had heard so distinctly during the whole banquet, no longer broke the silence.

'Well,' said the fisherman, 'that's a capper, in o mi born days. I see 'em as plain as a pikestaff. Th' last day connot be far off, I'm sewer. Bud I'll hev th' tabble, at onny rate, beawt axin.' And, so saying, he took possession of the huge mushroom, and after hurriedly gathering up his lines, he wended his way across the meadow to his little cottage by the high road, and arrived there, he narrated to his drowsy wife the story of the banquet.

'Drat th' fairies, an' thee, too, wi' thi gawmless tales,' said his sceptical helpmate, 'I wondered what hed getten tha. Tha's bin asleep for hours i' th' meadow istid a lookin' after th' fish. Tha never seed a fairy i' thi life. Tha'rt nod hauve sharp enough, clivver as tha art i' owt as is awkurt.' There was a short pause after this sally, and then the sly Reuben drily answered--

'Yoy, I 've sin a fairy monny an' monny a time. Olus when I used to come a cooartin' to thi moather's. Bud tha 'r nod mich like a fairy neaw, tha 'st autert terbly. Tha 'rt too thrivin' lookin'.'

'Be off wi' thi fawseness,' said the pleased woman; 'tha 'd ollus a desayvin tung i' thi heead;' and then after a drowsy pause as she was dosing to sleep; 'but for o that I'll mek a soop o' good catsup out o' thi fairy tabble.

'THE WHITE DOBBIE.

Many years ago, long before the lovely Furness district was invaded by the genius of steam, the villagers along the coast from Bardsea to Rampside were haunted by a wandering being whose errand, the purpose of which could never be learned, used to bring him at night along the lonely roads and past the straggling cottages. This pilgrim was a wearied, emaciated-looking man, on whose worn and wan face the sorrows of life had left deep traces, and in whose feverish, hungry-looking eyes, mystery and terror seemed to lurk. Nobody knew the order of his coming or going, for he neither addressed anyone, nor replied if spoken to, but disregarded alike the 'good neet' of the tramp who knew him not, and the startled cry of the belated villager who came suddenly upon him at a turn of the road. Never stopping even for a minute to gaze through the panes whence streamed the ruddy glow of the wood fires, and to envy the dwellers in the cosy cottages, he kept on his way, as though his mission was one of life and death, and, therefore, would not brook delay.

On wild wintry nights, however, when the salt wind whirled the foam across the bay, and dashed the blinding snow into heaps upon the window-sills and against the cottage doors, and darkness and storm spread their sombre wings over the coast, then was it certain that the mysterious being would be seen, for observation had taught the villagers and the dwellers in solitary houses along the lonely roads between the fishing hamlets that in storm and darkness the weird voyager was most likely to appear.

At such times, when the sound of footsteps, muffled by the snow, was heard between the soughs and moans of the wailing wind, the women cried, 'Heaven save us; 'tis th' White Dobbie,' as, convulsively clutching their little ones closer to their broad bosoms, they crept nearer to the blazing log upon the hearth, and gazed furtively and nervously at the little diamond-paned window, past which the restless wanderer was making his way, his companion running along a little way in advance, for not of the mysterious man alone were the honest people afraid. In front of him there invariably ran a ghastly-looking, scraggy white hare,{21} with bloodshot eyes. No sooner however did anyone look at this spectral animal than it fled to the wanderer, and jumping into his capacious pocket, was lost to sight.

Verily of an unearthly stock was this white hare, for upon its approach and long before it neared a village, the chained dogs, by some strange instinct conscious of its coming, trembled in terror, and frantically endeavoured to snap their bonds; unfastened ones fled no man knew whither; and if one happened to be trotting alongside its belated master as he trudged homeward and chanced to meet the ghastly Dobbie with its blood-red eyes, with a scream of pain almost human in its keen intensity, away home scampered the terrified animal, madly dashing over hedge and ditch as though bewitched and fiend-chased.

For many years the lonely wanderer had traversed the roads, and for many years had the hare trotted in front of him; lads who were cradled upon their mother's knee when first they heard the awe-inspiring footfalls had grown up into hearty wide-chested men, and men who were ruddy fishers when the pilgrim first startled the dwellers in Furness had long passed away into the silent land; but none of them ever had known the wayfarer to utter a syllable. At length, however, the time came when the solemn silence was to be broken.

One night when the breeze, tired of whispering its weird messages to the bare branches, and chasing the withered leaves along the lanes, had begun to moan a hushed prelude to the music of a storm, through the mist that had crept over the bay, and which obscured even the white-crested wavelets at the foot of the hill on which stood the sacred old church, there came at measured intervals the melancholy monotone of the Bardsea passing bell{9} for the dead.

Dismally upon the ears of the dwellers in the straggling hamlet fell the announcement of the presence of death, and even the woman who had for years been bell-ringer and sexton, felt a thrill of fear as she stood in the tower but dimly lighted by a candle in a horn lantern, and high above her head the message of warning rang out; for, although accustomed to the task, it was not often that her services were required at night. Now and again she gazed slowly round the chamber, upon the mouldering walls of which fantastic shadows danced, and she muttered broken fragments of prayers in a loud and terrified voice, for as the door had been closed in order that the feeble light in the lantern might not be extinguished by the gusts of wind, isolated as she was from the little world upon the hillside, she felt in an unwonted manner the utter loneliness of the place and its dread surroundings.

Suddenly she uttered a shrill shriek, for she heard a hissing whisper at her ear and felt an icy breath upon her cheek. She dared not turn round, for she saw that the door opening upon the churchyard remained closed as before, and that occasionally passing within the range of her fixed stare, a white hare with blood-red eyes gambolled round the belfry.

'T' Dobbie!' sighed she, as the dim light began to flicker and the hare suddenly vanished.

As she stood almost paralysed, again came the terrible whisper, and this time she heard the question--

'Who for this time?'

The horrified woman was unable to answer, and yet powerless to resist the strange fascination which forced her to follow the direction of the sound; and when the question was put a second time, in an agony of fear she gazed into the wild eyes of the being at her elbow, her parched tongue cleaving to her open mouth. From the pocket of the dread visitor the ghastly animal gazed at the ringer, who mechanically jerked the bell-rope, and the poor woman was fast losing her senses, when suddenly the door was burst open, and a couple of villagers, who had been alarmed by the irregular ringing, entered the tower. They at once started back as they saw the strange group--the wanderer with sad, inquiring look, and pallid face, the phantom hare with its firelit eyes, and the old ringer standing as though in a trance. No sooner, however, did one of the intruders gaze at the animal than it slipped out of sight down into the pocket of its companion and keeper, and the wanderer himself hastily glided between the astonished men, and out into the darkness of the graveyard.

On many other gloomy nights afterwards the ringer was accosted in the same manner, but although the unnatural being and the spectral hare continued for some winters to pass from village to village and from graveyard to graveyard, a thick cloud of mystery always hung over and about them, and no one ever knew what terrible sin the never-resting man had been doomed to expiate by so lonely and lasting a pilgrimage.

Whence he came and whither he went remained unknown; but long as he continued to patrol the coast the hollow sound of his hasty footsteps never lost its terror to the cottagers; and even after years had passed over without the usual visits, allusions to the weird pilgrim and his dread companion failed not to cause a shudder, for it was believed that the hare was the spirit of a basely-murdered friend, and that the restless voyager was the miserable assassin doomed to a wearisome, lifelong wandering.{22}

THE LITTLE MAN'S GIFT.

Many are the wells in Lancashire that once were supposed to be the homes of good or evil spirits--of demons or of beneficent fairies--and, despite the injunctions of the Church against the customs of praying at and waking wells, down to a comparatively recent period they were resorted to by pilgrims of all grades who were in search of health. One such spring near Blackpool, known as the Fairies' Well, had its daily crowds of the ailing and the sorrowful, for its water was credited with virtues as wonderful as they were manifold, and from far and near people brought vessels to be filled with the miraculous fluid.

One day at noon, a poor woman who had journeyed many a weary mile in order to obtain a supply of the water with which to bathe the eyes of her child, whose sight was fast failing, and upon whom all the usual remedies had been tried without success, on rising from her knees at the well side, was surprised to find standing near her a handsome little man clad in green, who certainly was not in sight when she bent to fill her bottle. As she stood gazing at the dainty object, the visitor, without having previously asked her any questions, handed to her a beautiful box filled with ointment, and directed her to apply the salve to the eyes of her child, whose sight it would restore. Surprised beyond measure at the little man's knowledge of her family affairs, the woman mechanically accepted the gift, but when, after carefully placing the box in her pocket, she turned to thank the giver, he was no longer to be seen; and satisfied that she had had an interview with one of the beings after whom the well was named, she started on her journey to her distant home.

The strangeness of the present, given as she trusted it was by a fairy who was conversant with the painful circumstances under which she had made her pilgrimage, caused her to hope that the ointment would prove efficacious in removing the disorder under which her child was labouring; but this vague feeling, based as it was upon the mysterious nature of the gift, was accompanied by a perfectly natural fear that, after all, the giver might have been one of those mischievous beings whose delight it was to wreak harm and wrong upon humanity.

When she reached home and told the strange story to her wondering husband, the nervous pair decided that the ointment should not be used unless a further mark of fairy interest in the child's welfare were vouchsafed to them; but when a few days had passed, and the child continued to grow worse, the anxious mother, in the absence of her husband, determined to test the salve upon one of her own eyes. She did so, and after a few minutes of dreadful suspense, finding that evil results did not follow, and saying to herself that surely the fairy could not be desirous of harming her child, she anointed the little girl's eyes. She refrained, however, from making her helpmate acquainted with what she had done, until in the course of a few days the child's eyesight was so nearly restored that it was no longer necessary or possible to keep the matter from him. Great were the rejoicings of the worthy pair over their little one's recovery; but there was not for a very long time any opportunity afforded them of expressing their gratitude.

Some years had passed,--and, as the girl had never had a relapse, the strange gift was almost forgotten,--when one day, in the market-place at Preston, the woman, who was haggling about the price of a load of potatoes, saw before her the identical little fellow in green attire from whom, long before, she had received the box of wonder-working ointment. Although he was busily engaged in a pursuit in which, perhaps, few gentlemen would care to be interrupted, that of stealing corn from an open sack, the thoughtless woman, regardless of etiquette, and yielding to the sudden impulse which prompted her to thank him, stepped forward, and, grasping the fairy's hand, gave utterance to her gratitude.

To her surprise, however, the little fellow seemed very angry with her, and, instead of acknowledging her thanks, hastily asked if she could see him with both eyes, and if she had used the ointment intended for her child. The frightened woman at once said that she saw him with only one eye, and was entering into a long account of the circumstances under which, with maternal instinct, she had tested the value of the gift, when, without more ado, the irritated fairy struck her a violent blow and vanished, and from that time forward the poor woman, instead of being able to see better than her neighbours, was blind of one eye. The daughter, however, often saw the fairies, but, profiting by her mother's painful experience, she was wise enough to refrain from speaking to them either when they gathered by moonlight beneath the trees or in broad daylight broke the Eighth Commandment, utterly unconscious that they were observed by a mortal to whom had been given the wondrous gift of fairy vision.{23}

SATAN'S SUPPER.{24}I.

 Ye Evil One
The 'Old Lad' sat upon his throne,
giveth untoBeneath a blasted oak,
them a stayve.And fiddled to the mandrake's groan, The marsh-
frog's lonely croak;
 II.
 Ye corpses
 Whilst winds they hissed, and shrieked, and moaned
dashe theirAbout the branches bare,
wigges. And all around the corpses groaned, And shook their
mould'ring hair;
III.
 Ye hagges
As witches gathered one by one,
crowde to ye
 And knelt at Satan's feet,
levee.With faces some all worn and wan, And some with features
sweet,
 IV.
 Ye powerThe earth did ope and imps upsprang
of
Of every shape and shade,
Musicke.Who 'gan to dance as th' welkin rang With tunes the 'Old
Lad' played;V.
 Ye poetrie
 At which the witches clapped their hands,
of
And laughed and screamed in glee;
motion. Or jumped about in whirling bands, And hopped in revelry,
 VI.
 Ye delicacies Till Satan ceased, when all did rest,
of yeAnd swarmed unto the meat:
season, The flesh of infants from the breast, The toes from dead
men's feet,
VII.
 Ye ditto,With sand for salt, and brimstone cates, With blood for old
wine red;On glittering dish and golden plates The dainty food was
spread.
VIII.
 YeFrom heavy cups, with jewels rough,
coolinge

The witches quenched their thirst;
drinkes.Yet not before the ruddie stuff Had been by Satan cursed.
 IX.
 Ye bardeBut one lank fiend of skin and bone,
telleth ofWith hungry-looking eyne,
an outcaste
Gazed at the food with dreary moans,
impe.And many a mournful whine;X.
 Of hys
For Satan would not let him feed
unparalleled
 Upon the toothsome cheer,
wickednesse;
(He had not done all day a deed To cause a human tear);
 XI.
 Of hys
And so he hopped from side to side,
gamboles
To beg a bit of 'toke,'
and praieres, And, vagrant-like, his plea denied, He prayed that
they might choke
XII.
 And of
Themselves with morsels rich and fat
hys Or die upon the floor,
revylyngs of
Like paupers (grieving much thereat
goode menne.
 The guardians of the poor).
XIII.
 Ye earlie byrdeA cock then flapped his wings and crew,
prepareth for ye Announcing coming light;
'Diet ofWhen, seizing on a jar of stew,
Wormes.'
The snubbed imp took his flight.
XIV.
 Les Adieux. And at the solemn sound of doom The witches flew
away,While Satan slunk off through the gloom, Afraid of break of
day;
 XV.
 Ye fruitlesse And in the darkness drear he cried--
remorse ofHis voice a trifle gruff,
Beelzebubbe.

'Those omelettes were nicely fried; I have not had enough!'
XVI.
 Ye resulte
 A blight fell on the trembling flowers
of ye meetynge
And on the quivering trees--
uponne yeNo buds there drink the passing showers, Or leaves wave
in the breeze;
XVII.
 Agryculture
For Satan's presence withered all
of yeThe daisies and the grass,
dystricte.
 And all things over which like pall His sulphurous tail did pass.

THE EARTHENWARE GOOSE.

Once upon a time, which somewhat vague reference in this instance means long before it was considered a compliment by the fair dames of Lancashire to be termed witches, there lived in the Fylde country village of Singleton a toothless, hooknosed old woman, whose ill fortune it was to be credited with the friendship of the Evil One. Perhaps had the ancient dame been somewhat better looking she might have borne a better character. In those distant days to be poor was considered decidedly discreditable, but to be ugly also was to add insult to injury. The old woman knew only too well that she was poor and that she was plain, for the urchins and hobbledehoys of the locality lost no opportunity of reminding her of the facts, whenever, on frugal mind intent, she emerged from her rude cottage to expend a few pence upon articles of food.

Ugliness and poverty, however, Mag Shelton persisted in considering misfortunes and not crimes, and when anybody to whom she was an eyesore, with gallantry peculiar to the time and place let us hope, wished that she would die and rid the village of her objectionable presence, the old woman took no notice of the polite expression. To die by particular desire was not in Mag's line. What harm could a toothless old woman do, that the world, by which term the half-dazed creature meant the village in which she had spent her life, should evince so much anxiety to be rid of her?-- argued Mag. True, if toothless, she had her tongue; but without a visiting circle, and with no benefactors to belie, that valuable weapon in the service of spite might just as well have been in the mouth of an uneducated heathen. Harmless, however, as the old dame thought herself, the villagers held a different opinion, and the children, afraid of disturbing the witch, invariably removed their wooden-soled clogs before they ran past the hut in which Mag lived,{25} while the older folk, if they did not literally take the coverings from their feet as they passed the lonely dwelling, crept by on tiptoe, and glanced furtively at the unsuspecting inhabitant of the cottage, who, by the aid of the fitful firelight, might be seen dozing near the dying embers, and now and again stroking a suspiciously bright-eyed cat, nestled snugly upon her knee.

The old woman's solitary way of life favoured the growth of superstitions regarding her, for the Singletonians were not without their share of that comforting vanity which impresses the provincial mind with a sense of the high importance of its society, parish, and

---

creed; and they could not imagine anyone preferring to keep away
from them and to sit alone, without at once believing, as a
necessary consequence, that the unappreciative ones must have
dealings with Satan.

It soon was found convenient to attribute anything and everything
of an unpleasant nature to the denizen of the lonely cottage, 'th'
Owd Witch,' as she was termed. Was a cow or a child ailing? Mag
had done it! Had the housewife omitted to mark with the sign of the
cross the baking of dough left in the mug on the hearth, and the
bread had turned out 'heavy,' Mag Shelton had taken advantage
of the overworked woman's negligence! Was there but a poor field
of wheat? 'Twas the fault of old Mag, swore the farmer. In short,
whatever went wrong throughout the entire country-side was
judged to be clearly traceable to the spite and malevolence of the
toothless old woman and her suspicious-looking cat.

This state of things might, however, have continued without any
interruption, until Nature had interposed and released Mag from her
attendance upon such a world, had it not begun to be noticed that
almost every farmer in the neighbourhood was complaining of the
mysterious disappearance of milk, not only from the dairies, but also
from the udders of the cows grazing in the pastures. A bucolic
genius immediately proclaimed that in this case, too, the culprit
must be Mag, for had not she her familiars to feed, and what could
be more agreeable to the palate of a parched fiend or perspiring
imp, than a beaker of milk fresh from the cow and redolent of
meadow-flowers? With such a gaping family to satisfy, what regard
could the old lady retain for the Eighth Commandment?

This logic was deemed unanswerable, and a number of the farmers
determined to conceal themselves one night about the witch's
cottage, in the hope of something confirmatory turning up. It was
late when they took their places, and they barely had settled
themselves comfortably behind the hedgerow before a noise was
heard, and the old woman emerged from the house,--the cat, and,
of all things else in the world, a stately goose solemnly paddling
behind her.

The men in ambush remained silent until Mag and her attendants
had passed out of sight and hearing, when one of them said, 'Keep
still, chaps, till hoo comes back. Hoo's gone a milkin', I daat.' The
watchers therefore kept perfectly quiet, and in a little while their

---

patience was rewarded; for the old woman reappeared, walking slowly and unattended by her former companions. As she paused to unfasten the cottage door, the men pounced out of their hiding-place, seized her roughly, and at once tore off her cloak. To the surprise of the rude assailants, however, no sign of milkjugs could be observed; and, as they stood aghast, Mag cried, in a shrill and angry voice, 'Will ye never learn to respect grey hair, ye knaves?' 'We'll respect tha' into th' pit yon, mi lady,' immediately responded one of the roughest of the men. 'What hes ta done with th' milk to-neet?'

In vain were the old woman's protestations,--that, driven from the roads and lanes in the daytime by the children and the hobbledehoys who persecuted her, she had of late taken her exercise by night; the judicial mind was made up, and rude hands were outstretched to drag her to the horsepond, when, fortunately for Mag, the appearance of the goose, waddling in a hurried and agitated manner, created a timely diversion in her favour.

'I thowt it quare,' said one of the would-be executioners--'varra quare, that th' goose worn't somewheer abaat, for hoo an' it's as thick as Darby an' Jooan.'

As though conscious that all was not well with its mistress, the ungainly and excited bird, stretching its neck towards the bystanders, and hissing loudly, placed itself by the old woman's side.

'We want no hissin' heear,' said the leader of the band, as he lifted a heavy stick and struck the sibilant fowl a sharp rap on its head.

No sooner had the sound of the blow fallen upon the ears of the assembled rustics than the goose vanished, not a solitary feather being left behind, and in its place there stood a large broken pitcher, from which milk, warm from the cow, was streaming. Here was proof to satisfy even the most credulous, and, as a consequence, in a moment the old woman was floundering in the pond, from which she barely escaped with her life. A few days afterwards, however, upon the interposition of the Vicar, she was permitted to leave the inhospitable village, and away she tramped in search of 'fresh woods and pastures new,' her cat and the revivified goose bearing her company.{26}

She had left the inhospitable place, when the landlord of the Blue Pig discovered that the jug in which the witch-watchers had conveyed their 'allowance' to the place of ambush had not been returned. It was not again seen in its entirety, and the sarcastic host often vowed that it was here and there in the village in the shape of cherished fragments of the broken one into which the watchers declared that they had seen Mag's goose transformed.

THE PHANTOM OF THE FELL.

On a beautiful night late in summer a solitary man, who was returning from some wedding festivities, was rapidly crossing Fair Snape. The moon was at the full, and threw her glamour upon the lovely fell, as a breeze sighed among the tall ferns which waved gently to and fro under the sweet invisible influence, and the only sounds which fell upon the wayfarer's ear were the almost inaudible rustling of the bracken, and the occasional faint bark of a distant watch-dog. Giles Roper, however, was not thinking of the beauty of the night, or of the scenery, but, naturally enough, was congratulating himself upon being ever so much nearer to the stocking of that farm without which he could not hope for the hand of the miller's rosy daughter. Thoughts of a chubby, good-hearted little woman like Liza were calculated to drive out all other and less pleasant ones; but Giles was rapidly approaching a part of the hillside said to be haunted. Many tales had he heard by the winter's fire of the doings of the nameless appearance, the narrators speaking in hushed voices, and the hearers instinctively drawing closer together on the old settle; and these narratives crowded into his recollection as he left the cheerful moonlight and stepped into the shade of the little clough. Before he had got very far down he was prepared to see or hear anything; but, making allowance for the fear which somehow or other had taken possession of him, he knew that there was something more than fancy in a melancholy wail which broke upon his ears as he reached a bend in the ravine. There was nothing however in the sad note of lamentation calculated to terrify, save the consciousness that such sweet music could not be that of a mortal. Instinctively Giles looked in the direction whence the sound had come, and in the dim light he saw the figure of a woman with a pallid face of singular and unearthly beauty, her hair falling behind her like a sheet of gold, and her eyes emitting a strange lustre, which, however, was not sufficiently intense to conceal their beautiful azure hue. The bewildered spectator gazed in rapt worship, for though his limbs still trembled he no longer felt any fear, but rather a wild delirious longing to speak to, and to be addressed by, the beautiful being before him. He was sufficiently near to the appearance to be able to distinguish the features clearly, and when he saw a movement of the lips his heart throbbed violently under the expectation that he was about to receive a mysterious commission. He was, however, doomed to be disappointed, for the only sound emitted by the phantom was another low melodious cry, even more pathetic and mournful than that by which his attention had first been attracted to the lovely object. At the same time Giles saw that the figure was more distant than before, and that it was slowly gliding away, but beckoning to him, as though anxious that he should follow. The young man, spell-bound and fascinated by the enchanting eyes, which were beautiful enough to turn the head of one wiser than the raw country lad upon whom they were fixed, followed eagerly, but at the end of the clough, where the moonlight was brilliant, the figure vanished, leaving Giles, not with that feeling of relief said to follow the disappearance of a mysterious visitant, but, on the contrary, anxious to behold the vision again. He therefore turned and retraced his steps to the undulating summit of the fell, where the wind was sighing over the many-flowered heather, but there was nothing to be seen of the blue-eyed phantom, and only for the faint wash of the rustling ferns all would have been silent.

Unwilling to leave the spot, although he was conscious that the task was a fruitless one, he continued to wander from one point to another, and it was not until daybreak that he finally gave up the search and descended the fell. Not caring to allude to his adventure and vain search upon the pike, Giles accounted for his lateness by asserting that he had remained until midnight at the distant farmhouse where the rejoicings had taken place, and had afterwards lost his way on the fells. With this excuse, however, his relatives were quite content, one sarcastic farm-servant drily remarking that after wedding festivities it was wonderful he had been able to find his way home at all.

The extraordinary thoughtfulness which Giles evinced during the day was of too marked a nature to remain unobserved; but the old father attributed it merely to that natural dislike to settled labour which generally follows boisterous relaxation, and the mother thought it was due to a desire to be off again to see the chubby daughter of the miller. The old dame, therefore, was not surprised when her son announced his intention to leave home for a few hours, and she congratulated herself on her foresight and discernment, finishing her soliloquy by saying--'Well, hoo's a bonny wench as he's after; an', what's mooar, hoo's as good as hoo's pratty.'

It was not, however, to the far-off dwelling of the miller that Giles was making his way.

On the contrary, he was leisurely pacing in quite an opposite
direction, his back turned to the old mill, and his eyes fixed upon the
distant fells, which he did not care to reach until the gloaming had
given way to moonlight. Not that he was afraid of being seen, the
road he trod was too lonely for that; but he thought it was unlikely his
watchings would be rewarded before the night had properly set in.
If the beautiful object was a spirit--and what else could it have
been?--it would come at its own time, and who ever heard of spirits
appearing before midnight? The young fellow, therefore, waited
until the moon rose and bathed the hills in her golden flood, when
he at once began to climb the fell, making his way up the ravine in
which on the previous night he had heard the mysterious voice.

It was some time from midnight, and he stopped to rest, taking his
seat upon a moss-covered stone. Here he waited patiently; but he
had begun to fear that his visit was to be a fruitless one, when once
more he heard the peculiar mournful wail, and rapidly turning round,
he saw that he was not alone. Again the weird eyes, in all their
unearthly beauty, were fixed upon him, and the long white arms
were extended as though to beckon him to draw nigh.

Instinctively Giles rose in obedience to the pleading attitude of the
fair vision; but as he approached the phantom it grew less and less
distinct, and at length vanished. As on the previous night, the young
fellow wandered about in the hope of again seeing the lovely
being, and once more he was obliged to return to the farm
unsuccessful.

Possessed by a maddening and irresistible desire to gaze upon the
wondrous face which had bewitched him, the approach of nightfall
invariably found Giles on his way to the fell, and it can easily be
imagined to what unpleasantness in his family circle this course of
conduct gave rise. On the one hand the parents gave the rein to all
sorts of vague suspicions as to the cause of the night rambles; and
the lad's disinclination to give any explanations did not help the old
people to think more kindly of him. The father of the girl whom he
had asked in marriage also did not fail to expostulate with him, in
the idea that he had fallen into evil ways, and that his pilgrimages
were to a distant town; while the girl herself, loving him as she did
with all the vigour of her simple and earnest nature, and
uninfluenced by any foolish feeling of false shame, came to his
parents' house in the hope of obtaining a promise of better things.

Her pleadings and her womanly threats, however, were unavailing, the whilom lover in a shamefaced manner refusing to make any promise of different behaviour. The interview was a painful one; for the girl, feeling certain that her father's interpretation was correct, used all her powers to induce Giles to abandon his evil courses; but at length, finding that her prayers were ineffectual, she bitterly reproached him with his want of honesty.

'It's no evil as I'm after, lass! Don't think that on mi,' said the young man, in an appealing tone; but the girl was not to be convinced by mere assertion.

'It's no good as teks tha away o'er t' pike neet after neet,' said she, with a sudden access of grief, 'it'ull come by tha in some way or another, Giles.' And in tears she turned away from him.

'Whisht, lass, whisht! If tha nobbut knew, O tha'd pity i'stid o' blaming mi.'

The girl heeded not these words, but kept on her way. When she got to a turn in the road, however, she looked back mournfully, as though in doubt whether to return and cast herself upon his breast, and bid him trust in her; but pride overcame her, and she resisted the impulse.

That night, as two of the miller's men were poaching, they were startled by the unexpected sound of a human voice, and hastily hiding themselves beneath the tall ferns, they saw Giles emerge from the clough and run towards the place where they were concealed. He seemed to be half mad with excitement, and as he ran he was crying aloud some words they could not catch. When he drew nearer, however, they were able to hear more distinctly, and to their surprise they found that he was appealing to an invisible being to appear to him.

For some time they remained in their place of concealment, Giles hovering about the spot; but when the young fellow ran to a distance, they emerged from their hiding-place and rapidly made their way to the mill. For obvious reasons, however, they agreed to keep silence as to what they had seen and heard.

The day after this episode Giles was in a fever and delirious, raving continually about the bonny face and 'breet een' of the being he had seen in the ravine. His afflicted parents found in the wild utterances sad confirmation of their worst fears, and, half broken-hearted, they hovered sorrowfully about his bed. For weeks he battled with the disorder, and at nightfall frequently endeavoured to leave the house, and vainly struggled with the friends who prevented him, to whom he frantically cried that she of the blue eyes was calling him.

A cloud fell over the hitherto happy household. Night and day the old people watched over their sick lad, each of them feeling that the task would have been a comparatively easy one had not the patient's delirious ravings revealed to them so terrible a background to the round of their primitive and innocent daily life. Not that they loved their child any less because of the revelations he had unconsciously made to them, but they brooded and fretted over his supposed wickedness, and bowed their heads in grief and shame as they unwillingly heard his impassioned cries.

By-and-by the story of these ravings got noised about, and the miller's daughter, who hitherto had been suffering bravely, broke down altogether when she knew that she was an object of pity to the gossips. It fortunately happened, however, that the miller's men who had seen Giles at the pike got into conversation with their master about the matter, and it struck one of them that the woman about whom Giles was supposed to be raving, and of whom tales of all sorts were being circulated, was a feeorin of some kind that the young fellow had seen on the lonely fell. No sooner was this idea arrived at than off they started to see the distressed parents, the miller's daughter hastening with them. They found no difficulty in gaining credence for their narrative, and with a burst of thankfulness the old people felt that the gulf which had yawned between them and their eldest born was for ever closed; while, as for the girl, her transports of joy were almost painful in their intensity. So great a weight was lifted from all hearts that the illness of the patient was for the time almost forgotten. Giles, however, still remained in a very critical condition, but he soon had an additional nurse, who, despite the watchings and the toil of which she relieved the old people, was rapidly becoming more and more like the ruddy-faced damsel to whom the young fellow had plighted his troth, for she could listen to and disregard the ravings of her lover and look forward to the time when happiness should again smile upon them.

A few weeks passed. The violence of the disorder abated, and the patient recovered so far as to be able to bear removal to a large chair by the kitchen fire. As he sat quietly dreaming the short autumn days away, without any allusions to the beauty about whom he had so constantly raved during his delirium, the old people and the miller's daughter began to congratulate themselves that the dream-madness had passed away with the worst phase of the illness. The girl, however, although she did not utter any complaint, suffered deeply from the coolness with which Giles treated her. Not that he was ungrateful, for, on the contrary, it was impossible to do anything for him, however slight the service might be, without a thankful acknowledgment; but there was a visible constraint in his manner which could not escape the keen sight of love. Fearing to distress him by any remonstrances, the patient girl refrained from referring to the past or showing that she was observant of any change in his behaviour towards her, but she brooded over her grief when she was alone. The young fellow knew that the poor girl was suffering, but for the life of him he could not assume that which he did not feel. Much as he had loved her before the night of his adventure on the pike, from the moment when he had first seen the face of the mysterious being his affection for her had faded away, consumed by the intense longing which filled his soul night and day whenever he thought of the eyes illumined by a fire that was not human, and of the features and hair so exquisitely beautiful in the faint moonlight. Calm and quiet as he looked, seated propped with cushions in the old chair by the fire, he was inwardly fretting against the weakness that kept him from the fells, and his longing soul came into his eyes as he gazed through the little diamond-paned window, and saw the pike, in all the beauty of many-tinted autumn, kissed by the setting sun as the blushing day sank into the swarthy arms of night.

Slowly winter came, bringing snow and storm, and as though influenced by a feeling that even Nature had interposed her barriers between him and the lovely being, one afternoon, as the mists crept slowly over the white landscape, and hid in their shimmering folds the distant fells where he had first seen the sweet face so seldom absent from his feverish dreams, he could not resist the desire which seized him to visit once more the haunted ravine. The various members of the little household were away from the house engaged in their labours about the farm, and taking advantage of this, Giles fled from the dwelling, and made his way through the dim light to the hills. It was not long, however, before his absence was discovered, but some time elapsed before the men-folk could be gathered, and the shades of night had fallen before the anxious pursuers reached the foot of the pike.

The thick mist had enveloped everything, and as the lanterns, choked as they were by the damp, threw but a fitful light, it was with the utmost difficulty that the men found the footmarks of the wanderer in the snow up the fell side. The searchers were led by the father of Giles, who spoke not, but glanced at the track as though in dread of discovering that which he had come to find. Suddenly the old man gave a startled cry, for he had followed the marks to the edge of a little cliff, over which he had almost fallen in his eagerness. It was forthwith determined to follow the ravine to its commencement, and although nothing was said by any of the party, each man felt certain that the missing young fellow would be found at the bottom. It did not take long to reach the entrance, and with careful steps the old man led the way over the boulders. He had not gone far before the light from his lantern fell upon the upturned face of his son, whose body lay across the course of a little frozen stream. The features were set in the sleep of death, for Giles had fallen from the level above, the creeping mists having obscured the gorge where he first saw the lovely phantom, in search of which he had met an untimely end.

ALLHALLOW'S NIGHT.

To many a beautiful landscape the majestic Pendle adds a nameless charm, and the traveller who gazes upon it from any of the points whence a view of the whalelike mass is to be obtained, would hardly dream that the moss and fern-covered hill, smiling through the dim haze, once was the headquarters of witchcraft and devilry. Readers of the quaint and sad trials of the witchmania period, and of Harrison Ainsworth's celebrated novel based thereon, will, however, remember what dread scenes were said to have transpired in the dim light of its cloughs and upon its wild sides, when Chattox, Mouldheels, and the other poor wretches whose 'devilish practices and hellish means,' as they were termed in the old indictments, made the neighbourhood of the mountain so unsafe a locality.

In a lonely little house some distance from the foot of Pendle, there dwelt a farmer and his family, together with a labourer whom he employed. Entirely illiterate, and living in a wild and weird district, with but few houses nearer than a mile away, the household believed firmly in all the dreadful boggart, witch, and feeorin stories current in the district. For a long time, however, the farmer had not any personal experience of the power of either witch or boggart; but at length his turn came. After a tempestuous night, when the windows and doors rattled in their frames, and the wind, dashing the big rain drops against the little diamond-shaped panes, moaned and shrieked round the lonely dwelling, three of the beasts were found dead in the shippon. A few days afterwards two of the children sickened, and when 'th' edge o' dark' was creeping up the hill-side one of them died. As though this trouble was not enough, the crops were blighted. With reluctance the farmer saw in these things proof that he had in some unknown manner incurred the displeasure of the invisible powers, and that the horse-shoe over his door, the branches of ash over the entrance to the shippon, and the hag stones hung up at the head of his own and of the children's bed, had lost their power of protection.

The family council, at which the unprotected condition of the house was discussed, was of the saddest kind, for even the rough labourer missed the prattle of the little one whose untimely end had cast a shadow over the dwelling, and he thoroughly sympathised with his master in his losses; while, as for the farmer and his wife, dread of what the future might have in store for them mingled with their

---

sorrow, and added to the heaviness of their hearts.

'Isaac, yo' may as weel tek' th' wiggin{27} an' th' horse shoes deawn, for onny use they seem to be on. We'en nowt to keep th' feorin' off fra' us, an' I deawt we'es come off bud badly till November,' said the farmer, as he knocked the ashes from his pipe.

'An' why nobbut till November, Ralph,' asked the wife in a terrified voice, as she gazed anxiously towards the little window through which Pendle could be dimly seen looming against the evening sky.

'Because on O'Hallow neet, mi lass, I meean to leet th' witches{28} on Pendle.'

'Heaven save us!' cried the woman. 'Tha'll be lost as sewer as th' whorld.'

There was a short silence, and then old Isaac spoke--

'If th' mestur goes, Isik guz too. Wis be company, at onny rate.'

The farmer gratefully accepted this offer of fellowship, and the appeals of his wife, who implored him to abandon the notion, were of no avail. Others had lighted the witches, and thereby secured a twelvemonth's immunity from harm, and why should not he go and do likewise? Ruin was staring him in the face if things did not improve, thought he, and his determination to 'leet' his unseen enemies grew stronger and stronger.

At length the last day of October came, bringing with it huge clouds and a misty rain, which quite obscured the weird hill; but at nightfall the wind rose, the rain ceased, the stars began to appear, and the huge outline of Pendle became visible.

When the day's work was over, the farmer and Isaac sat in the kitchen, waiting for the hour at which they were to start for the haunted mountain, and the dread and lonesome building where the witches from all parts gathered in mysterious and infernal conclave. Neither of the men looked forward to the excursion with pleasurable feelings, for, as the emotion caused by the losses had somewhat subsided, terror of the beings who were supposed to assemble in the Malkin Tower resumed its sway; but soon after the old clock had chimed ten they rose from the settle and began their preparations for the lighting. Each man grasped a branch of mountain ash, to which several sprigs of bay were tied as a double protection against thunder and lightning, and any stray fiends that might happen to be lurking about, and each carried in the other hand an unlighted candle.

As they passed from the house the tearful goodwife cried a blessing upon them, and a massive old bulldog crept from a corner of the yard and took its place at their heels.

The three stepped along bravely, and before long they had crossed the brook and reached the foot of Pendle. Rapidly making their way to a well-known ravine they paused to light the candles. This operation, performed by means of a flint and steel and a box of tinder, occupied some time; and while they were so engaged clouds obscured the moon, a few heavy drops of rain fell, the wind ceased to whisper, and an ominous silence reigned, and the dog, as though terrified, crept closer to its master and uttered a low whine.

'We's hev' a storm, I daat, Isik,' said the farmer.

'Ise think mysen weel off an' win nowt else bud a storm,' drily replied the old man, as, lighted candle in hand, he began to climb the hill-side, his master and the dog following closely behind.

When they had almost reached the top of the ravine a flash of lightning suddenly pierced the darkness, and a peal of thunder seemed to shake the earth beneath them; while a weird and unearthly shriek of laughter rang in their ears as a black figure flew slowly past them, almost brushing against their faces in its flight. The dog immediately turned and fled, howling terribly as it ran down the hill-side; but the men went on, each one carefully shading his light with the hand in which the branch of ash was grasped. The road gradually became rougher, and occasionally Isaac stumbled over a stone, and almost fell, the farmer frantically shouting to him to be careful of his candle, but without any serious mishap the pair managed to get within sight of the tower.

Evidently some infernal revelry was going on, for light streamed from the window-openings, and above the crash of the thunder came shrieks of discordant laughter. Every now and again a dark figure floated over their heads and whirled in at one of the windows, and the noise became louder, by the addition of another shrill voice.

'It mon be drawin' nee midneet,' said the farmer. 'If we con but pass th' hour wis be reet for a twelvemonth. Let's mek for whoam neaw.'

Both men readily turned their backs to the building, but no sooner had they done so than a Satanic face, with gleaming eyes, was visible for a moment, and instantaneously both lights were extinguished.

'God bless us!' immediately cried both men.

Almost before the words had left their lips the tower was plunged in total darkness, the shrieks of unholy laughter were suddenly stilled, and sounds were heard as of the rapid flight of the hags and their familiars, for the ejaculations had broken up the gathering.

Terrified beyond measure at the extinction of their lights, but still clinging tenaciously to the branches, which apparently had proved so ineffectual to preserve them against the power of the witches, the men hurried away. They had not proceeded far in the direction in which they supposed the farm lay, when, with a cry, the farmer, who was a little in advance of his aged companion, fell and vanished. He had slipped down the cleft, on the brink of which Isaac stood, tremblingly endeavouring to pierce the darkness below.

Not a sound came up to tell the old man that his master had escaped with his life; and, as no response came to his shouts, at length he turned away, feeling sure that he was masterless, and hoping to be able to reach the farm, and obtain assistance. After wandering about for some time, however, half-blinded by the lightning, and terrified beyond measure at the result of their mutual boldness, Isaac crept under a large stone, to wait for the dawn. Influenced by the cold and by fatigue, the old man fell asleep; but no sooner had the first faint rays of coming day kissed the hill-summit, than he was aroused by the old bulldog licking his face, and as he gazed around in sleepy astonishment some men appeared. The farmer's wife, terrified by the arrival of the howling dog, and the non-arrival of the 'leeters,' had made her way to a distant farm-house and alarmed the inmates, and a party of sturdy fellows had started off to find the missing men. Isaac's story was soon told; and when the searchers reached the gorge the farmer was found nursing a broken leg.

Great were the rejoicings of the goodwife when the cavalcade
reached the farm, for, bad as matters were, she had expected
even a worse ending; and afterwards, when unwonted prosperity
had blessed the household, she used to say, drily, 'Yo' met ha' kept
th' candles in to leet yo' whoam, for it mon ha' bin after midneet
when _he_ blew 'em aat,' a joke which invariably caused the farmer
and old Isaac to smile grimly.

THE CHRISTMAS-EVE VIGIL.

Many years have passed since the living of Walton-le-Dale was held
by a gentleman of singularly-reserved and studious habits, who, from
noon till night, pored over dusty black-letter folios. Although he was
by no means forgetful of the few duties which pertained to his
sacred office, and never failed to attend to the wants of those of his
parishioners who were in trouble and had need of kind words of
sympathy and advice, or even of assistance of a more substantial
nature, the length of time he devoted to his mysterious-looking
volumes, and a habit he had of talking to himself, as, late at night,
with head bent down, he passed along the village street, and
vanished into the darkness of a lonely lane, gave rise to cruel
rumours that he was a professor of the black art; and it was even
whispered that his night walks were pilgrimages to unholy scenes of
Satanic revelry. These suspicions deepened almost into certainty
when the old people who had charge of his house informed the
gossips that the contents of a large package, since the arrival of
which the women in the village had been unable to sleep for
curiosity, were strange-looking bottles, of a weird shape, with awful
signs and figures upon them; and that, during the evening, after the
carrier had brought them, noises were heard in the clergyman's
room, and the house was filled with sulphurous smoke. Passing from
one gossip to another, the story did not fail to receive additions as
usual, until when it reached the last house in the straggling village
the narrator told how the student had raised the Evil One, who, after
filling the house with brimstone, vanished in a ball of fire, not,
however, without first having imprinted the mark of his claws upon
the study table.

Had the unconscious clergyman lived more in the everyday world
around him, and less in that of black-letter books, he would not
have failed to perceive the averted looks with which his parishioners
acknowledged his greetings, or, what would have pained him even
more deeply, the frightened manner in which the children either fled
at his approach, if they were playing in the lanes, or crept close to
their parents when he entered the dwellings of the cottagers.
Ignorant alike of the absurd rumours, and unobservant of the
change which had come over his flock, or at least acting as though
unaware of them, the clergyman continued to perform the duties of
his sacred office, and to fly from them to his beloved volumes and
experiments, growing more and more reserved in his habits, and
visibly paling under his close application.

After matters had gone on in this way for some time, the villagers were surprised to see a friendship spring up and ripen between their pastor and an old resident in the village, of almost equally strange habits. There was, however, in reality but little to wonder at in this, for the similarity between the pursuits and tastes of the two students was sufficiently great to bridge over the gulf of widely-different social positions.

Abraham, or 'Owd Abrum,' as he was generally named, was a herb doctor, whose knowledge of out-of-the-way plants which possessed mysterious medicinal virtues, and of still more wonderful charms and spells, was the theme of conversation by every farmhouse fireside for miles round. At that day, and in that locality, the possession of a few books sufficed to make a man a wonder to his neighbours; and Abraham had a little shelf full of volumes upon his favourite subjects of botany and astrology.

The old man lived by himself in a little cottage, some distance along a lane leading from the village across the meadows; and, despite the absence of female supervision, the place always was as clean and bright as a new pin. Had he needed any assistance in his household duties, Abraham would not have asked in vain for it, for he was feared as well as respected. If he was able to charm away evil and sickness, could he not also bring sickness and evil? So reasoned the simple villagers; and those who were not, even unconsciously, influenced by the guileless everyday life of the old man, were impressed by the idea that he had the power to cast trouble upon them if they failed to maintain an outward show of reverence.

However early the villagers might be astir, as they passed along the lanes on their way to their labour in the fields, they were certain to find 'Owd Abrum' searching by the hedgerows or in the plantations for herbs, to be gathered with the dew upon them; and at night the belated cottager, returning from a distant farm, was equally certain of finding Abraham gazing at the heavens, 'finding things aat abaat fowk,' as the superstitious country people said and believed.

Addicted to such nocturnal studies, it was not likely that the old herb doctor and the pale student would remain unknown to each other. The acquaintance however, owing to the reserved habits of both, began in a somewhat singular manner. Returning from a long and

late walk about midnight, the minister was still some distance from
his abode, when he heard a clear voice say: 'Now is the time, if I
can find any: Jupiter is angular, the moon's applied to him, and his
aspect is good.'

The night was somewhat cloudy--the stars being visible only at
intervals--and it was not until the clergyman had advanced a little
way that he was able to perceive the person who had spoken. He
saw that it was the old herbalist, and immediately accosted him. An
animated conversation followed, Abraham expatiating on the
virtues of the plants he had been gathering under the dominion of
their respective planets, and astonishing the pale student by the
extent of his information. In his turn, the old man was delighted to
find in the clergyman a fellow-enthusiast in the forbidden ways of
science; and as the student was no less charmed to discover in the
'yarb doctor' a scholar who could sympathise with him and
understand his yearnings after the invisible, late as was the hour, the
pair adjourned to Abraham's cottage. The visitor did not emerge
until the labourers were going to their toil, the time having been
spent in conversation upon the powers exercised by the planets
upon plants and men, the old man growing eloquent as to the
wonderful virtue of the Bay Tree, which, he said, could resist all the
evil Saturn could do to the human body, and in the neighbourhood
of which neither wizard nor devil, thunder or lightning, could hurt
man; of Moonwort, with the leaves of which locks might be opened,
and the shoes be removed from horses' feet; of Celandine, with
which, if a young swallow loseth an eye, the parent birds will renew
it; of Hound's Tongue, a leaf of which laid under the foot will save
the bearer from the attacks of dogs; of Bugloss, the leaf of which
maketh man poison-proof; of Sweet Basil, from which (quoting
Miraldus) venomous beasts spring--the man who smelleth it having a
scorpion bred in his brain; and of a score of other herbs under the
dominion of the Moon and Cancer, and of the cures wrought by
them through antipathy to Saturn.

From that time the pair became intimate friends, the clergyman
yielding, with all the ardour of youth, to the attraction which drew
him towards the learned old man; and Abraham gradually growing
to love the pale-faced student, whose thirst after knowledge was as
intense as his own. Seldom a day passed on which one of them
might not have been observed on his way to the abode of the
other; and often at night the pair walked together, their earnest
voices disturbing the slumbering echoes, as at unholy hours they

---

passed up the hill, and through the old churchyard, with its moss-covered stones and its rank vegetation.

Upon one of these occasions they had talked about supernatural appearances; and as they were coming through the somewhat neglected God's Acre, the clergyman said he had read, in an old volume, that to anyone who dared, after the performance of certain ghastly ceremonies, wait in the church porch on Christmas-eve, the features of those who were to die during the following year would be revealed, and that he intended upon the night before the coming festival to try the spell. The old man at once expressed a wish to take part in the trial, and before the two parted it was agreed that both should go through the preliminary charms, and keep the vigil.

In due time the winter came, with its sweet anodyne of snow, and as Christmas approached everything was got in readiness.

Soon after sunset on Christmas-eve the old herb doctor wended his way to the dwelling of his friend, taking with him St. John's Wort, Mountain Ash, Bay leaves, and Holly. The enthusiasts passed the evening in conversation upon the mysterious qualities of graveyard plants; but shortly after the clock struck eleven they arose, and began to prepare for the vigil, by taking precautions against the inclemency of the weather, for the night was very cold, large flakes of snow falling silently and thickly upon the frozen ground.

When both were ready the old man stepped to the door to see that the road was clear, for, in order to go through the form of incantation, a small fire was requisite; and as they were about to convey it in a can, they were anxious that the strange proceeding should not be noticed by the villagers. Late as it was, however, lights shone here and there in the windows, and even from the doorways, for, although it was near midnight, many of the cottage doors were wide open, it being believed that if, on Christmas-eve, the way was thus left clear, and a member of the family read the Gospel according to St. Luke, the saint himself would pass through the house.

As the two men, after carefully closing the door behind them, stepped into the road, a distant singer trolled forth a seasonable old hymn. This was the only noise, however, the village street being deserted. They reached the churchyard without having been observed, and at once made their way round the sacred building, so as not to be exposed to the view of any chance reveller returning to his home. It was well that they did so, for they had hardly deposited the can of burning charcoal upon a tombstone ere sounds of footsteps, somewhat muffled by the snow, were heard, and several men passed through the wicket. They were, however, only the ringers, on their way to the belfry, and in a few minutes they had entered the building, and all was still again for a few moments, when, upon the ears of the somewhat nervous men there fell the voices of choristers singing under the window of a neighbouring house the old Lancashire carol--'As I sat anonder yon green tree,Yon green tree, yon green tree--As I sat anonder yon green treeA Christmas day in the morning.'{29}

The words could be heard distinctly, and almost unconsciously the two men stood to listen; but directly the voices ceased the student asked if they had not better begin, as the time was passing rapidly.

'Ay,' replied Abraham, 'we han it to do, an' we'd better ger it ower.'

Without any more words they entered the porch, and at once made a circle around them with leaves of Vervain, Bay, and Holly. The old man gave to his companion a branch of Wiggintree,{27} and firmly held another little bough, as with his disengaged hand he scattered a powder upon the embers. A faint odour floated around them, as they chanted a singular Latin prayer; and no sooner was the last word uttered than a strain of sweet sad music, too inexpressibly soft and mournful to be of earth, was heard. Every moment it seemed to be dying away in a delicious cadence, but again and again was the weird melody taken up by the invisible singers, as the listeners sank to their knees spell-bound. An icy breath of wind hissed round the porch, however, and called the entranced men to their senses, and suddenly the student grasped the arm of his aged companion, and cried, in a terrified voice--

'Abraham, the spell works. Behold!'

The old man gazed in the direction pointed out, and, to his inexpressible horror, saw a procession wending its way towards the porch. It consisted of a stream of figures wrapped up in grave-clothes, gleaming white in the dim light. With solemn and noiseless steps the ghastly objects approached the circle in which stood the venturesome men, and, as they drew nearer, the faces of the first two could be seen distinctly, for the blazing powder cast a lurid glow upon them, and made them even more ghastly.

Both spectators had almost unconsciously recognised the features of several of the villagers, when they were aroused from their lethargy of terror by the appearance of one face, which seemed to linger longer than its predecessors had done. Abraham at once saw that the likeness was that of the man by his side, and the clergyman sank to the ground in a swoon.

For some time the old man was too much affected by the lingering face to think of restoring the unconscious man at his feet; but at length the clashing of the bells over his head, as they rang forth a Christmas greeting, called him to himself, and he bent over the prostrate form of his friend. The minister soon recovered, but as he was too weak to walk, the old man ran to the belfry to beg the ringers to come to his assistance. When these men came round to the porch the fire was still burning, the flickering flames of various colours casting dancing shadows upon the walls.

'Abraham,' said one of the ringers, 'there's bin some wizzard wark goin' on here, an' yo' sin what yo'n getten by it.'

'Han yo' bin awsin to raise th' devul, an' Kesmus-eve an' o'?' asked another, in a low and terrified voice.

With a satirical smile, Abraham answered the last speaker: 'It dusn't need o' this mak' o' things to raise th' devul, lad. He's nare so far fra' thuse as wants him.'

Bearing the clergyman in their arms, the men walked through the village, but they did not separate without having, in return for the confidence Abraham reposed in them by confiding to them the secret of the vigil, promised strict secrecy as to what they had witnessed.

Abraham's companion soon recovered from the shock, but not before the story of the night-watch had gone the round of the village. Many were the appeals made to the old herbalist to reveal his strangely-acquired knowledge, but Abraham remained sternly obdurate, remarking to each of his questioners--

'Yo'll know soon enough, mebbi.'

The clergyman, however, was in a more awkward position, and his parishioners soon made him aware how unwise he had been in giving way to the desire to pry into futurity; for, when any of them were ill and he expressed a kindly wish for their recovery, it was by no means unusual for the sick person to reply--

'Yo could tell me heaw it will end iv yo' loiked.'

This oftentimes being followed by a petition from the assembled relatives--

'Will yo tell us if he wir one o' th' processioners?'

Ultimately Abraham's companion went away, in the hope of returning when the memory of the watch should have become less keen, but, before a few months had passed away, news came of his death, after a violent attack of fever caught during a visit to a wretched hovel in the fishing village where he was staying. By the next December, all the people whose features the old herbalist had recognised during the procession had been carried to the churchyard; but, although several men offered to accompany Abraham to the porch on the forthcoming Christmas-eve, he dared not again go through the spells and undergo the terrors of a church-porch vigil.{30}

THE CRIER OF CLAIFE.

Upon a wild winter night, some centuries ago, the old man who plied the ferry-boat on Windermere, and who lived in a lonely cottage on the Lancashire side of the Lake, was awakened from his sleep by an exceedingly shrill and terrible shriek, which seemed to come from the opposite shore. The wind was whistling and moaning round the house, and for a little while the ferryman and his family fancied that the cry by which they had been disturbed was nothing more than one of the mournful voices of the storm; but soon again came another shriek, even more awe-inspiring than the former one, and this was followed by smothered shouts and groans of a most unearthly nature.

Against the wishes of his terrified relatives, who clung to him, and besought him to remain indoors, the old fellow bravely determined to cross the water, and heeding not the prayers of his wife and daughter, he unfastened his boat, and rowed away. The two women, clasped in each other's arms, trembling with fear, stood at the little door, and endeavoured to make out the form of their protector; but the darkness was too deep for them to see anything upon the lake. At intervals, however, the terrible cry rang out through the gloom, and shrieks and moans were heard loud above the mysterious noises of the night.

In a state of dreadful suspense and terror the women stood for some time, but at length they saw the boat suddenly emerge from the darkness, and shoot into the little cove. To their great surprise, however, the ferryman, who could be seen sitting alone, made no effort to land, and make his way to the cottage; so, fearing that something dreadful had happened to him, and, impelled by love, they rushed to the side of the lake. They found the old man speechless, his face as white and blanched as the snow upon the Nab, and his whole body trembling under the influence of terror, and they immediately led him to the cottage, but though appealed to, to say what terrible object he had seen, he made no other response than an occasional subdued moan. For several days he remained in that state, deaf to their piteous entreaties, and staring at them with wild-looking eyes; but at length the end came, and, during the gloaming of a beautiful day, he died, without having revealed to those around him what he had seen when, in answer to the midnight cry, he had rowed the ferry-boat across the storm-ruffled lake.

After the funeral had taken place the women left the house, its associations being too painful to permit of their stay, and went to live at Hawkshead, whence two sturdy men, with their respective families, removed to the ferry. The day following that of the arrival of the new-comers was rough and wild, and, soon after darkness had hidden everything in its sable folds, across the lake came the fearful cry, followed by a faint shout for a boat, and screams and moans. The men, hardy as they were, and often as they had laughed at the story told by the widow of the dead man, no sooner heard the first shriek ring through the cottage than they were smitten with terror. Profiting, however, by the experience of their predecessor, and influenced by fear, they did not make any attempt to cross the lake, and the cries continued until some time after midnight.

Afterwards, whenever the day closed gloomily, and ushered in a stormy night, and the wind lashed the water of the lake into fury, the terrible noises were heard with startling distinctness, until at length the dwellers in the cottage became so accustomed to the noises as not to be disturbed by them, or, if disturbed, to fall asleep again after an ejaculation of 't' crier!' Pedlars and others who had to cross the lake, however, were not so hardened, and after a time the ferry-boat was almost disused, for the superstitious people did not dare to cross the haunted water, save in the broad daylight of summer.

It therefore struck the two individuals who were most concerned in the maintenance of the ferry that if they intended to live they must do something to rid the place of its bad name, and of the unseen being who had driven away all their patrons. In their extremity they asked each other who should help them, if not the holy monks, who had come over the sea to the abbey in the Valley of Deadly Night Shade; and one of the ferrymen at once set out for Furness. No sooner had he set eyes upon the stately pile erected by the Savignian and his companions than his heart felt lighter, for he had a simple faith in the marvellous power of the white-robed men, whose voices were seldom if ever heard, save when lifted in worship during one of their seven daily services.

Knocking at the massive door, he was received by a ruddy-looking servitor, who ushered him into the presence of the abbot. The ferryman soon told his story, and begged that a monk might return with him to lay the troubled spirit, and after hearing the particulars of the visitation, the abbot granted the request, making a proviso, however, that the abbey coffers should not be forgotten when the lake was freed from the fiend.

No sooner had the visitor finished the meal set before him by the hospitable monks than, in company with one of the holy men, he set out homeward. As, by a rule of his order, the monk was not permitted to converse, the journey was not an enlivening one, and the ferryman was heartily glad when they reached his cottage.

The first night passed without any alarm, the monk and his hosts spending the dreary hours in watching and waiting. The following day, however, was as stormy as the worst enemy of the ferry could have wished, and, when night fell, all the dwellers in the cottage, as well as the silent monk, gathered together again to wait for the cries, but some hours passed without any other sounds having been heard than those caused by the restless wind, as it swept over the lake and among the trees. The Cistercian was beginning to imagine himself the victim of an irreverent practical joke, and that the stories of the spectral crier which had reached the distant abbey long before the ferryman's visit were a pack of falsehoods, when about midnight, he suddenly jumped from the chair upon which he was dozing by the wood fire, hastily made the sign of the cross, and hurriedly commended himself to the protection of his patron saint, for sharp and clear came the dread cry, followed rapidly by a number of shrieks and groans and a smothered appeal for a boat.

In an instant one of the men, with courage doubtless inspired by the presence of the holy man, shouldered the oars and opened the door, and the monk at once stepped into the open air and hurried to the lake, the men following at a respectful distance. The white-robed father was the first to get into the boat, and the ferrymen hoped that he intended to go alone, but he called upon them to propel the boat to the middle of the lake, and much as they disliked the task, as it was on their behalf that the monk was about to combat the evil spirit, they could not well refuse to accompany him.

When they were about half-way across the lake the wind suddenly lulled, and once more they heard the awful scream, and this time it sounded as though the crier was quite close to them. The occupants of the boat were terribly frightened, and one of them, after suddenly shrieking 'he's here,' fainted, and lay still at the bottom of the boat, while the monk and the other man stared straight before them, as though petrified.

There was a fourth person present, a grim and ghastly figure, with the trappings of this life still dangling about its withered and shrunken limbs, and a gaping wound in its pallid throat. For a few minutes there was a dead silence, but at last it was broken by the monk, who rapidly muttered a prayer for protection against evil spirits, and then took a bottle from a pocket of his robe, and sprinkled a few drops of holy water upon himself and the ferryman, who remained in the same statuesque attitude, and upon the unconscious occupant of the bottom of the boat. After this ceremony, he opened a little book, and, in a sonorous voice, intoned the form for the exorcism of a wandering soul, concluding with _Vade ad Gehennam!_ when to the infinite relief of the ferryman, and probably of the monk also, the ghastly figure forthwith vanished.

The Cistercian asked to be immediately taken to the shore, and when he neared the house, the little book was again brought into requisition, and the spirit's visits, should it ever again put in an appearance, limited to an old and disused quarry, a distance from the cottage.{31}

From that time to this, the wild, lonely place has indeed been desolate and deserted, the boldest people of the district not having sufficient courage to venture near it at nightfall, and the more timid ones shunning the locality even at noonday. These folks aver that even yet, despite the prayers and exorcisms of the white-robed Cistercian from Furness, whenever a storm descends upon the lake, the Crier escapes from his temporary prison house, and revisits the scene of his first and second appearance to men, and that on such nights, loud above the echoed rumble of the thunder, and the lonely sough of the wind, the benighted wayfarer still hears the wild shrieks and the muffled cry for a boat.

THE DEMON OF THE OAK.

Once a fortress and a mansion, but now, unfortunately, little more than a noble ruin, Hoghton Tower stands on one of the most commanding sites in Lancashire. From the fine old entrance-gate a beautiful expanse of highly-cultivated land slopes down and stretches away to the distant sea, glimmering like a strip of molten silver; and on either hand there are beautiful woods, in the old times 'so full of tymber that a man passing through could scarce have seen the sun shine in the middle of the day.' At the foot of these wooded heights a little river ripples through a wild ravine, and meanders through the rich meadows to the proud Ribble. From the building itself, however, the glory has departed. Over the noble gateway, with its embattled towers, and in one of the fast-decaying wainscots, the old family arms, with the motto, _Mal Gre le Tort_, still remain; but these things, and a few mouldering portraits, are all that are left there to tell of the stately women who, from the time of Elizabeth down to comparatively modern days, pensively watched the setting sun gild the waters of the far-off Irish Sea, and dreamed of lovers away in the wars--trifling things to be the only unwritten records of the noble men who buckled on their weapons, and climbed into the turrets to gaze over the road along which would come the expected besieging parties. Gone are the gallants and their ladies, the roystering Cavalier and the patient but none the less brave Puritan, for, as Isaac Ambrose has recorded, during the troublous times of the Restoration, the place, with its grand banqueting chamber, its fine old staircases, and quaint little windows, was 'a colledge for religion.' The old Tower resounds no more with the gay song of the one or the solemn hymn of the other, 'Men may come, and men may go,'

and an old tradition outlives them all.

To this once charming mansion there came, long ago, a young man, named Edgar Astley. His sable garments told that he mourned the loss of a relative or friend; and he had not been long at the Tower before it began to be whispered in the servants'-hall that 'the trappings and the suits of woe' were worn in memory of a girl who had been false to him, and who had died soon after her marriage to his rival. This story in itself was sufficient to throw a halo of romance around the young visitor; but when it was rumoured that domestics, who had been returning to the Tower late at night, had seen strange-coloured lights burning in Edgar's room, and that, even at daybreak, the early risers had seen the lights still unextinguished, and the shadow of the watcher pass across the curtains, an element of fear mingled with the feelings with which he was regarded.

There was much in the visitor calculated to deepen the impressions by which the superstitious domestics were influenced, for, surrounded by an atmosphere of gloom, out of which he seemed to start when any of them addressed him, and appearing studiously to shun all the society which it was possible for him to avoid, he spent most of his time alone, seated beneath the spreading branches of the giant oak tree at the end of the garden, reading black-letter volumes, and plunged in meditation. Not that he was in any way rude to his hosts; on the contrary, he was almost chivalrous in his attention to the younger members of the family and to the ladies of the house, who, in their turn, regarded him with affectionate pity, and did their utmost to wean him from his lonely pursuits. Yet, although he would willingly accompany them through the woods, or to the distant town, the approach of the gloaming invariably found him in his usual place beneath the shadow of the gnarled old boughs, either poring over his favourite books, or, with eyes fixed upon vacancy, lost in a reverie.

Time would, the kind people thought, bring balm to his wounds, and in the meanwhile they were glad to have their grief-stricken friend with them; and fully appreciating their sympathy, Edgar came and went about the place and grounds just as the whim of the moment took him. This absence of curiosity on the part of the members of the family was, however, amply compensated for by the open wonder with which many of the domestics regarded the young stranger; and before he had been many months in the house his nightly vigils were the theme of many a serious conversation in the kitchen, where, in front of a cosy fire, the gossips gathered to compare notes.

Unable to repress their vulgar curiosity, or to gratify it in any more honourable or less dangerous manner, it was determined that one of the domestics should, at the hour of twelve, creep to the door of the visitor's chamber, and endeavour to discover what was the nature of those pursuits which rendered lights necessary during the whole of the night. The selection was soon made, and after a little demur the chosen one agreed to perform the unpleasant task.

At midnight, therefore, the trembling ambassador made his way to the distant door, and after a little hesitation, natural enough under the circumstances, he stooped, and gazed through a hole in the dried oak whence a knot had fallen. Edgar Astley was seated at a little table, an old black-looking book with huge clasps open before him. With one hand he shaded his eyes from the light which fell upon his face from the flames of many colours dancing in a tall brazen cup. Suddenly, however, he turned from his book, and put a few pinches of a bright-looking powder to the burning matter in the stand. A searching and sickly odour immediately filled the room, and the quivering flames blazed upwards with increased life and vigour as the student turned once more to the ponderous tome, and, after hastily glancing down its pages, muttered: 'Strange that I cannot yet work the spell. All things named here have I sought for and found, even blood of bat, dead man's hand, venom of viper, root of gallows mandrake, and flesh of unbaptized and strangled babe. Am I, then, not to succeed until I try the charm of charms at the risk of life itself? And yet,' said he, unconscious of the presence of the terrified listener, 'what should I fear? So far have I gone uninjured, and now will I proceed to the triumphant or the bitter end. Once I would have given the future happiness of my soul to have called her by my name, and now what is this paltry life to me that I should hesitate to risk it in this quest, and perhaps win one glimpse of her face?'

There was a moment of silence as the student bent his head over the book, but though no other person was visible, the listener, to his horror, quickly heard a sharp hissing voice ask, 'And wouldst thou not even yet give thy soul in exchange for speech with thy once betrothed?' The student hastily stood erect, and rapidly cried: 'Let me not be deceived! Whatever thou art, if thou canst bring her to me my soul shall be thine now and for ever!'

There was a dead hush for a minute or two, during which the lout at the door heard the beating of his own heart, and then the invisible being again spoke: 'Be it so. Thou hast but one spell left untried. When that has been done thou shalt have thy reward. Beneath the oak at midnight she shall be brought to thee. Darest thou first behold me?'

'I have no fear,' calmly replied the student, but such was not the state of the petrified listener, for no sooner had the lights commenced to burn a weird blue than he sank fainting against the door.

When he came to consciousness he was within the awful room, the student having dragged him in when he fell.

'What art thou, wherefore dost thou watch me at this hour, and what hast thou seen?' sternly demanded Edgar, addressing the terrified boor, and in few and trembling words the unhappy domestic briefly answered the queries; but the student did not permit him to leave the chamber, through the little window of which the dawn was streaming, before he had sworn that not a word as to anything he had seen or heard should pass his lips. The solemnity of the vow was deepened by the mysterious and awful threats with which it was accompanied, and the servant, therefore, loudly protested to his fellows that he had not seen or heard anything, but that, overcome by his patient watching, he had fallen asleep at the door; and many were the congratulations which followed when it was imagined what the consequences would have been had he been discovered in his strange resting-place.

The day following that of the adventure passed over without anything remarkable beyond the absence of Edgar from his usual seat under the shade of the giant oak, but the night set in stormily, dark clouds scudded before the wind, which swept up from the distant sea, and moaned around the old tower, whirling the fallen leaves in fantastic dances about the garden and the green, and shaking in its rage even the iron boughs of the oak. The household had retired early, and at eleven o'clock only Edgar and another were awake. In the student's chamber the little lamp was burning and the book lay open as usual, and Edgar pored over the pages, but at times he glanced impatiently at the quaint clock. At length, with a sigh of relief, he said, sternly and sadly, 'The time draws nigh, and once more we shall meet!' He then gathered together a few articles from different corners of the room and stepped out upon the broad landing, passed down the noble old staircase, and out from the hall. Here he was met by a cold blast of wind, which shrieked round him, as though rejoicing over its prey; and as Edgar was battling with it, a man emerged from a recess and joined him.

The night was quite dark, not a star or a rift in the sky visible, and the two men could hardly pick their way along the well-known path. They reached the oak tree, however, and Edgar placed the materials at its foot, and at once, with a short wand, drew a large circle around the domestic and himself. This done, he placed a little cauldron on the grass, and filled it with a red powder, which, although the wind was roaring through the branches above, immediately blazed up with a steady flame.

The old mastiffs chained under the gateway began to howl dismally; but, regardless of the omen,{32} Edgar struck the ground three times with his hazel stick, and cried in a loud voice: 'Spirit of my love, I conjure thee obey my words, and verily and truly come to me this night!'

Hardly had he spoken when a shadowy figure of a beautiful child appeared, as though floating around the magic ring. The servant sank upon his knees, but the student regarded it not, and it vanished, and the terrified listener again heard Edgar's voice as he uttered another conjuration. No sooner had he begun this than terrible claps of thunder were heard, lightning flashed round the tree, flocks of birds flew across the garden and dashed themselves against the window of the student's chamber, where a light still flickered; and, loud above the noises of the storm, cocks could be heard shrilly crowing, and owls uttering their mournful cries. In the midst of this hubbub the necromancer calmly went on with his incantation, concluding with the dread words: 'Spirit of my love, I conjure thee to fulfil my will without deceit or tarrying, and without power over my soul or body earthly or ghostly! If thou comest not, then let the shadow and the darkness of death be upon thee for ever and ever!'

As the last word left his lips the storm abated its violence, and comparative silence followed. Suddenly the little flame in the cauldron flared up some yards in height, and sweet voices chanting melodiously could be heard. 'Art thou prepared to behold the dead?' asked an invisible being.

'I am!' undauntedly answered Edgar.

An appearance as of a thick mist gathered opposite him, and slowly, in the midst of it, the outlines of a beautiful human face, with mournful eyes, in which earthly love still lingered, could be discerned.

Clad in the garments of the grave, the betrothed of Edgar Astley appeared before him.

For some time the young man gazed upon her as though entranced, but at length he slowly extended his arms as though to embrace the beautiful phantom. The domestic fell upon his face like one stricken by death, the spectre vanished, and again the pealing thunder broke forth.

'Thou art for ever mine,' cried a hissing voice; but as the words broke upon the ears of the two men, the door of the mansion was flung open, and the old baronet and a number of the servants, who had been disturbed by the violence of the storm, the howling of the dogs, and the shrill cries of the birds, rushed forth.

'Come not near me if ye would save yourselves,' cried the necromancer.

'We would save thee,' shouted the old man, still advancing. '_In nomine Patris_,' said he, solemnly, as he neared the magic circle; and no sooner had the words left his lips than sudden stillness fell upon the scene; the lightning no longer flashed round the oak; and, as the flame in the cauldron sank down, the moon broke through a cloud, and threw her soft light over the old garden.

Edgar was leaning against the oak tree, his eyes fixed in the direction where the image of his betrothed had appeared; and when they led him away, it was as one leads a trusting child, for the light of reason had left him. The unfortunate domestic, being less sensitive, retained his faculties; but he ever afterwards bore upon his wrist, as if deeply burned into the flesh, the marks of a broad thumb and fingers. This strange appearance he was wont to explain to stray visitors, by saying that when, terrified almost out of his wits, he fell to the ground, his hand was outside the magic circle, and 'summat' seized him; which lucid explanation was generally followed up by an old and privileged servitor, who remarked, 'Tha'll t'hev mooar marks nor thuse on tha' next toime as _He_ grabs tha', mi lad.

THE BLACK COCK.

'Ay,' said Old 'Lijah, 'I mind one time when they said th' Owd Lad hissel appear't i' broad dayleet, an' wir seen bi hunderts o' fowk, owd an' yung.'

There was a dead silence for a little while as the listeners gathered nearer the blazing fire, two or three of them getting a little further away from the door, against which the wind was dashing the snow, and then 'Lijah resumed: 'When I wir a lad, me an' mi mestur wer ast to a berryin. Ther wer a deeol o' drink stirrin, th' coffee pot, wi th' lemon peel hangin aat, gooin abaat fray one side to th' tother fast enough, and at last o' wer ready, but just as they wer baan to lift th' coffin a clap o' thunder shuke th' varra glasses o' th' table.

'Th' chaps as hed howd stopped a bit an' lukt raand, but th' deead chap's feythur shouted, "Come on, lads, or wist be late, an' th' paason waynt berry;" so they piked off, but no sooner hed they getten' i' th' street nor a lad i' th' craad cried out, "Heigh, chaps, luk at th' black cock {34} on th' top o' th' coffin," an' sure enough theer it wor. One o' th' beerers said directly as they'd enough to carry wi'out ony passingers, an' up wi' his fist an' knockt it off, but it wer on ageean in a minit, an one bi' one they o' hed a slap at it, but every time it wer knockt off back it flew to it' place at th' deead mon's feet, so at last th' owd mon give th' word of command, an' off they startit wi' th' looad. Th' craad geet bigger afooar they reached th' owd country church wheer he hed to be berried, an' th' fowk geet a throwin stooans at th' black bird, an' hittin it wi' sticks an' shaatin at it, but it stuck theer like a fixter.

'After a while we reached th' graveyart, an' th' paason come deawn th' road fray th' church door to meet th' coffin, an' he wer just baan to start th' service when he see th' bird an' stopped.

'"What han yo' got theere?" he says, lukin varra vext, for he thowt some marlock wer gooin on. "What han yo' theere, men?"

'Th' owd feythur stepped forrut an' towd him what hed happent, an' as nooan on 'em could freetun it off it peeark naythur wi' sticks or stooans or sweearin.

'"It's a strange tale," said th' vicar, "but we moant hev no brids here! Yo' fowk keep eaut o' th' graveyart nobbut thuse as is invitet to th' funeral! I'll settle him for yo!" an' so sayin he grabbed howd o' th' cock, an' walked o'er th' graves wi' it to a place wheer th' bruk run under th' hedges, an' then he bent deawn o' th' floor an' dipped th' bird i'th' watter, an' held it theer for abaat a quarter ov an hour.

'No sooner had he getten up, heawever, nor th' brid flew up eaut o' th' watter quite unhort, an' hopped o'er th' grass to th' coffin an' peearkt ageean as if nowt hed happent.

'Th' vicar lukt varra consarnt for a while, an' skrat his yed as he staret at th' fowk.

'Theer's summat not reet abaat that brid,' he said, 'but that's no rayson why we shouldn't bury th' deead!' an' he pottert off toart th' grave, an' th' beerers carriet th' coffin to th' side, an' th' sarvice wer gone through, wi' th' bird harkenin every word like a Christian.

'Th' chaps then startit o' lowerin th' coffin into th' grave, an' th' brid still stuck o' th' peeark, an' it wer nobbut when th' hole wer filled, as it came above graand ageean, an' theer it set on th' maand.

'A craad o' fowk waited abaat an' hung on th' graveyart wo' till th' edge o' dark, an' then they piket off whoam, for they begun to think as mebbi it were th' Owd Lad hissel, but a twothree on us stopped till it wer neet afooar we went after 'em, th' cock sittin theear just th' same as it hed done i' th' dayleet.

'It were usual i' thuse days to watch th' graves for a few neets, for ther wer a deeal o' resurrectionin' gooin on i'o' directions, th' body-snatchers hevin mooar orders than they could attend to; but though th' deead chap's feythur offert brass an' plenty o' drink an' meyt to anybody as ud keep a look aat, not one dar do it, an' th' deead mon wer laft to tek care o' hissel, or for th' brid to mind him.

'Soon after dayleet th' next mornin I went wi' a twothree moor young chaps to see heaw th' place lukt, an' th' grave hedn't bin brokken into, but th' brid had flown, and fray that day to this I could never find aat ayther wheer it coom fray or went to, but I heeart as th' vicar said it met be th' Owd Lad claimin' his own.

THE INVISIBLE BURDEN.

At the junction of the four cross roads, gleaming white in the hot sunshine and hawthorn-bounded, and marked by the parallel ruts made by the broad wheels of the country carts, the old public house of the _Wyresdale Arms_ was scarcely ever without a number of timber wagons or hay carts about its open door, the horses quietly munching from the nose-bags and patiently waiting until their owners or drivers should emerge from the sanded kitchen.

Nathan Peel's hostelry was the half-way house for all the farmers and cart-drivers in the district, and generally quiet enough at night time, but from its capacious kitchen roars of laughter rang out many a summer afternoon, as the carters and yeomen told their droll stories.

On one of these occasions, when the sun was blazing outside, and shimmering upon the sands and the distant sea, and through the open window the perfume of the may-blossom stole gently, a quaint looking old fellow, whose face had been bronzed by three-score summers and winters, happened to mention an occurrence as having taken place about the time of 'th' quare weddin','' and a chorus of voices at once called upon him for the story.

'It's quite forty year sin,' he said thoughtfully, 'an' I wir quite a young chap then, an' ready for any marlock. I could dance too wi' hear an' thear one, an' no weddin' wir reet wi'aat axin' me. This one I'm baan to tell abaat heawivir wir Mester Singleton's owdest son o' th' Dyke Farm, an' as he wir weddin' th' prattiest lass i' o' th' country side, varra nigh everybody wir theear, 'specially as Mester Singleton hed given it aat ther'd be a welcome for onnybody. A string o' nearly twenty conveyances, milk carts, an' shandrys, an' gigs, went to th' church wi' fowk o' seein' 'em wed; but comin' back, young Adam started off wi' his young wife as if he wir mad, an' isted o' gooin' th' owd road across th' Stone Brig, an' through th' Holme meadow he pelted off through th' Ingleton Road an' th' Owd Horse Lane. Th' mare seemed to know what th' young chap wir up to, an' to enter into th' spirit o't' thing an' off hoo went like th' woint, th' string o' shandrys an' milk carts an' gigs peltin' on at after abaat a mile behint, an' th' fowk laughin' an' shaatin' at th' fun. Th' gate into th' Owd Horse Lane wir wide open, so th' fowk wir disappointed as expected to gain a minnit or two wi' Adam hevin' to get daan theer to oppen it, an' into th' lane th' mare dashed, an' on hoo went as if th' shandry an' Adam an' his wife wir nowt behint her. Abaat midway i'th' lane heawever th' road dipped a bit, an' th' watter fra a spring i'th' bank ran o'er it, an' just afoor th' shandry reyched it th 'mare stopped o' of a sudden, an' Adam flew aat o'er th' horse's back an' pitched into th' hedge like leetnin'. Th' wife shaated as if he wir kilt, but he'd no bones brokken, an' when we geet up to him he crept aat o'th' prickles wi' a shame-faced look as if he'd bin catcht thievin'. Ther wir some rare jokin' as he climbed up to th' side of his wife an' lasht the mare for another start, but it wir no use, th' mare couldn't stir th' conveyance. Adam lasht away at her, but stir it hoo couldn't, an' at last eight or ten on us set to an' turned th' wheels for twenty or thirty yards an' it wir th' same as if it wir a timber-wagon, it wir that heavy. It wir th' same wi' every one o'th' conveyances, not one could be got o'er th' watter only wi' eight or ten on us toilin' an' slavin' at th' wheels, no matter heaw th' horse strained an' pulled. Nobody could make aat what it wir, an' th' Vicar came an' look't abaat but could find nowt. He said, heawever, th' Owd Lad had some hand in it, an' he warned th' fowk not to use th' road when they could help it. Many an' many a time heawivir, I see carts stuck theear bi' th' day together, for some chaps wouldn't be persuaded not to go through th' lane, for it wir a short cut, an' other chaps went i' nowt but darin' when they'd hed a sup o' drink. It went on for some years like that, an' fowk came fray far an' near to see it. I'd gettin' wed mysen and hed a farm on the Holme, but I used to go raand to it bi'th' owd road across the Brig, but one day, a breet hot day, I'd mi little lad i'th cart an' he bothert mi to go through th' lane, he wantit to see th' Owd Lad he said, an' as he started o' cryin' abaat it, I went. Well, the cart stuck i'th' owd place bi th' runnin' watter, an' th' little lad wir deleeted. I geet daan an' took howd o'th' wheel, for I knew it wir no use usin' the whip, an' th' horse wir sweatin' as if it wir rare an' 'freetont, when little Will shaated aat o' ov a sudden 'Feythar, I con see him!' 'See what?' I sang aat, an' broad dayleet as it wir, mi knees wir quakin'. 'A little chap i'th' cart,' he said, 'a fat little chap wi' a red neet cap on.' 'Wheer is he?' I shaated, for I couldn't see owt. 'Theer on th' cart tail,' he said, an' then he shaated 'Why, he's gone,' an' no sooner hed he spokken than th' horse started off wi' th' cart as if it hed nowt behint it.

Thir never wir a cart stuck theer at after that, an' th' Vicar said it wir because little Will hed persayved th' Feeorin, an' as Will hed th' gift o' seein' feeorin an' sich like because he wir born at midneet.

APPENDIX.

1.

Belief in the appearance of the Skriker, Trash, or Padfoot, as the
apparition is named in Lancashire, or Padfooit, as it is designated in
Yorkshire, is still very prevalent in certain parts of the two counties.
This boggart is invariably looked upon as the forerunner of death,
and it is supposed that only the relatives of persons about to die, or
the unfortunate doomed persons themselves, ever see the
apparition.

Of quite a distinct class to that of the 'Skrikin' Woman,' an
appearance which, at a but recent period, obtained for a lane at
Warrington the reputation of being haunted, the Padfoot seems to
be peculiar to Lancashire and Yorkshire, unless, indeed, the Welsh
Gwyllgi or Dog of Darkness, and the Shock of the Norfolk seaboard,
are of the same family. In Norfolk, the spectre, as it does in
Lancashire, portends death, but I have been unable to find any
Welsh story of the apparition with a more tragic ending than fright
and illness.

As the Trash generally takes the form of a large shaggy dog or small
bear, can the superstition be an offshoot from that old Aryan belief
which gave so important an office to the dog as a messenger from
the world of the dead, and an attendant upon the dying, or has the
grim idea come down to us from the ancient times, when, as the
Rev. S. Baring Gould says, 'It was the custom to bury a dog or a boar
alive under the corner-stone of a church, that its ghost might haunt
the neighbourhood, and drive off any who would profane it--_i.e._
witches or warlocks'?

2.

In most of these stories of compacts with the Evil One it is singular
how little is received in exchange for the soul. In a few instances
poverty bargains for untold wealth, or ugliness and age for youth
and loveliness, but generally it is for the bare means of prolonging or
supporting life that the daring and despairing one enters into the
everlasting agreement. In fact, as a French authoress has said, it is
'for a mouthful of bread to nourish their debilitated stomachs, and

the bundle of sticks which warms again their benumbed limbs.' In Sussex it would appear, from what a country-lad told the Rev. S. Baring Gould, that half-a-crown is the price Satan pays for a soul,--a letter addressed to the Evil One, and containing an offer of the soul, bringing a response in that practical form, if placed under the pillow at night.

In Normandy it is considered sufficient to make the compact binding for the acceptance to be simply a verbal one; but in Lancashire the formal parchment deed, with its signatures in blood, is indispensable.

3.

Old Isaac, it would seem, was not disappointed when he came to make use of his handful of money, and probably, therefore, he had spent it before he told the story, for in all instances where the fairies are recorded as rewarding mortals with money, any revelation as to its source is invariably followed by the gift being turned to bits of paper or leaves.

4.

Although there appears to have been some little confusion in the mind of the old farmer as to the rank in the world of faerie held by his little benefactor, he seems to have designated him correctly, for although the general idea of Puck is that of a mere mischief-loving and mischief-working sprite, such as is painted by Drayton, Shakspere credits Puck not only with wanton playfulness, but also with industry, for in the second act of the 'Midsummer Night's Dream,' the fairy, addressing the sprite, says:'Those that hobgoblin call you, and sweet Puck,_You do their work_.'

Shakspere and Ben Jonson, however, agree in making Oberon King of the Fairies--a king, too, with a stately presence, and far above showing an interest in a farmer's fields. Under any circumstances one is not prepared to find Puck of royal estate, and doubtless the labouring spirit of our story was simply one of those goblins who, according to the author of the _Anatomy of Melancholy_, would 'grind corn for a mess of milk, cut wood, or do any manner of nursery work'--a Robin Goodfellow merely, the 'lubber fiend' of Milton, the Bwbach or household fairy of Wales. Lancashire had many such. Stories of beings rejoicing in the name of Hobthrust or Throbthrush, but in all other respects closely resembling the fairy king of the

foregoing tradition, still are told by the farm-house fires in Furness, in
South-East Lancashire, and in the Fylde country. Rewarded night
after night with a supply of oatmeal porridge--strange relic,
probably, of the old libations to the gods--they toiled at the churn till
daybreak. A Furness legend chronicles how a farmer, whose house
was the favourite resting-place of one of these visitors, one evening,
when threatening clouds were gathering, wished that he had the
harvest carted. Next morning the work was found done, but a horse
was found dead in the stable, Hob having been unsparing. As the
day was a beautiful one, the farmer did not appreciate the housing
as he ought to have done, and testily wished that Hob was in the
mill-dam. A few hours afterwards, not Hob, but the grain was found
there.

'Crawshaws in Berwickshire,' says the author of the _Popular Rhymes
of Berwickshire_, 'was once the abode of an industrious Brownie,
who both saved the corn and thrashed it for several seasons. At
length, after one harvest, some person thoughtlessly remarked that
the corn was not well mowed or piled up in the barn. The sprite took
offence at this, and the next night threw the whole of the corn over
the Raven Crag, a precipice about two miles off, muttering--"It's no
weel mowed! It's no weel mowed!Then it's ne'er be mowed by me
again.I'll scatter it o'er the Raven stone,And they'll hae some wark
ere it's mowed again."'

The North Lancashire Hobthrusts, however, do not seem to have
been made to disappear by man's ingratitude, but, like the Irish
Cluricaun and the Scotch Brownie, were to be driven away by
kindness. In one instance, a tailor, for whom a Hobthrust had done
some work, gratefully made him a coat and hood for winter wear,
and in the night the workman was heard bidding farewell to his old
quarters--'Throb-thrush has got a new coat and new hood,And he'll
never do no more good.'

Readers of the Brothers Grimm and lovers of George Cruikshank will
not need to be reminded how the grateful shoemaker deprived
himself of the assistance of the elves. In the German story, however,
as in Breton ones, although the elves depart, prosperity continues to
bless the labours of the people whose practical gratitude has driven
the little beings away.

The Hob which, according to Harrison Ainsworth, haunted the Gorge
of Cliviger, does not appear to have been at all domesticated, the

novelist, in the only allusion he makes to it, characterising it as 'a frightful hirsute demon, yclept Hobthrust.' In the Fylde country, however, the lubber fiends seem to have been as industrious as was that of our legend. Tradition tells of one at Rayscar which not only housed the grain but also got the horses ready for the journey to the distant market. At Hackensall Hall one took the Celtic form of a great horse, and required only a pie in reward for its toil.

The Hobs of the neighbouring county of Yorkshire are credited with greater powers than those required for the rapid performance of household duties. One of these beings is still said to haunt a cave in the vicinity of the old-world hamlet of Runswick. To this place anxious and superstitious mothers brought their ailing little ones, and as they stood at the mouth of the cavity, cried, 'Hob, my bairn's gettent kinkcough (whooping-cough?), takkt off, takkt off!' In the same district there is a haunted tumulus called 'Obtrash Roque,' rendered by Walcott 'the Heap of Hob-o'-the-Hurst.' Of the bogle denizen of this mound a story similar to that told by Mr. Crofton Croker, in Roby's _Traditions (Clegg Hall Boggart)_, is current in the district. A farmer who was bothered by the spirit, determined to remove to a quieter locality, and as the carts were leaving with the goods and implements a neighbour cried out, 'It's flittin yo' are,' when the Hob at once replied, from a churn, 'Ay, we're flitting;' upon which the farmer thought he might as well remain where he was. Similar flitting stories, however, are told of the Scandinavian _Nis_, the Irish _Cluricaun_, the Welsh _Bwbach_, and the Polish _Ickrzycki_.

5.

Why the expression of a wish like this should have offended Puck is not very evident. There is in Sweden a lubber fiend named the _Tomte_, and of this being the peasantry believe that only by unrewarded toil can it work out its salvation. Can the Lancashire King of the Fairies have been one of the same order, and have considered the utterance of a good wish as a reward, or even as a sarcastic allusion to his 'lost condition'?

The belief is by no means uncommon that the fairies are the angels who were neutral during the Satanic rebellion. In Brittany, however (_Chants Populaires de la Bretagne_, par Th. Hersart de la Villemarqué), they are the Princesses who, in the days of the Apostles, would not embrace Christianity.

The traditions of most countries agree, however, in attributing to the fairies extreme sensitiveness on the subject of their condition. Mr. Campbell has recorded that when the elves, who had grown weary of crossing the Dornoch Frith in cockle-shells, were engaged in building a bridge of gold across its mouth, a passer-by lifted his hands and blessed the tiny workmen, who immediately vanished, the bridge sinking with them beneath the waves, and its place being at once taken by quicksands. Almost every district haunted by 'greenies' or 'hill folk' has its story of a piteous appeal on the subject of their future state made by visible or invisible fairies. In a Highland story it is an old man reading the Bible who is accosted, the inquirer screaming and plunging into the sea upon being answered that the sacred pages did not contain any allusion to the salvation of any but the sons of Adam. My friend, Mr. Kennedy, in his valuable _Legendary Fictions of the Irish Celts_, gives a charming traditionary story of a priest who was benighted and lost upon a moor, and who was similarly accosted, and implored to declare that at the last day the lot of the fairies would not be with Satan. After the appeal had been somewhat ambiguously answered, 'a weak light was shed around where he stood, and he distinguished the path and an opening in the fence.'

In Cornwall they are supposed to be the spirits of the people who inhabited the country long before the birth of Christ, and who, although not good enough to partake of the joys of Heaven, yet are too good for Hell. In Wales there is a somewhat similar belief, but it is said that their probation will end at the day of judgment, when they will be admitted to Paradise. It is commonly believed by the Cornish peasants that they are gradually growing smaller, and that at length they will change into ants. Few people in Cornwall, therefore, are sufficiently venturesome to destroy a colony of those insects.

6.

Many are the old sacred piles in Lancashire with the building of which it is believed that goblins had something to do. The parish church of Rochdale, the old church of Samlesbury, that of St. Oswald's at Winwick, near Warrington, and the parish church of Burnley, may be instanced as a few of those which are popularly supposed to have been interfered with by superhuman labourers. At Rochdale the unexpected workpeople took the form of 'strange-looking men;' in other cases, as in those of Winwick and Burnley, pigs removed the materials, it being traditional that their cry of 'we-week' gave its name to the former place; while at Newchurch, in Rossendale, although the interloping builders were invisible, a little old woman with a bottle was not only seen, but was fraternised with by the thirsty watchers who had been appointed to guard the foundations. Similar stories of changed site are told of numerous churches throughout Britain. The legend of Gadshill church, near Ventnor, like that of Hinderwell, Yorkshire, attributes the removal of the foundations to supernatural means, the stones having hopped after each other from their original place at the foot of the hill to that in which they were afterwards found, the shins of the watchers having been 'barked' in the most unceremonious manner by certain little blocks of somewhat erratic tendencies. It is, however, by no means improbable that at Gadshill, as at Rochdale, the fact of the building having been erected in a position so difficult of access, and so trying to aged and infirm parishioners, may have caused a testy and irreverent, and perhaps asthmatic, worshipper to invent the Satanic theory. In one case, that of Bredon, in Leicestershire, the objectors appear to have taken the form of doves. Loth as one may be to think harm of such sweet messengers, Mr. Kennedy, after telling the story of the building of the cathedral of Ardfert, in Kerry, by St. Brendain, and the trouble caused by a large crow, which took the measuring line in its bill and flew across the valley with it, adds, 'The bird was a fairy in disguise. If the messenger had been _from another quarter_, he would have made his appearance under snowy plumes.'[B]

[B] The foundations of the priory church of Christchurch, Hampshire, were, tradition says, removed by unseen hands, down from the lonely St. Catherine's Hill to the present site in the valley. The beams and rafters, too short on the hill, were too long in the vale. In the valley, too, an extra workman, Christ, always came on the pay-night.

7.

This work of art was one of the gargoyles of the old building, and was purchased by Mr. Ffarington, the father of the present lady of the manor, when the church was rebuilt. It bore the name of 'the Cat Stone.'

Another version of this tradition, of but limited circulation, and little known even in the immediate locality, credits an angel with the removal of the foundations and with the utterance of the following anything but angelic strain:--Here I have placed thee, And here shalt thou stand;And thou shalt be called The church of Leyland!

8.

This legend appears to have had a Teutonic origin. Mr. Kelly, in his chapter on the 'Wild Hunt,' quotes a somewhat similar story from a German source: 'The wild huntsman's hounds can talk like men. A peasant caught one of them, a little one, and hid it in his pack. Up came the wild huntsman and missed it. "Where are you, Waldmann?" he cried. "In Heineguggeli's sack," was the answer.'

9.

'The passing bell,' says Harland, 'according to Grose, was anciently rung for two purposes, one to bespeak the prayers of all good Christians for a soul just departing, the other to drive away the evil spirits who stood at the bed's foot ready to seize their prey, or at least to molest and terrify the soul on its passage.'

Mr. Sikes says that in Wales, before the Reformation, 'there was kept in all Welsh churches, a handbell which was taken by the Sexton to the house where a funeral was to be held, and rung at the head of the procession,' and that 'the custom survived long after the Reformation in many places, as at Caerleon, the little Monmouthshire village, which was a bustling Roman city when London was a hamlet. The bell, called the _bangu_, was still preserved in the parish of Llanfair Duffryn Clwyd half a dozen years ago.'

The bell might now with greater propriety be called the _passéd_ bell, as it is tolled only after a death, the ringing concluding with a number of distinct knells to announce the years and sex of the deceased, which the authority alluded to above considers 'a vestige of an ancient Roman Catholic injunction.' Until a comparatively recent period it was customary at Walton-le-Dale, Lancashire, to inter Protestants in the afternoon, a bell being tolled at intervals prior to the funeral; Catholics, however, were buried in the evening, a full peal being rung upon the bells immediately before the procession started.

Mr. Thornber, writing in 1844, says that at the beginning of this century, at Poulton, the more respectable portion of the inhabitants were buried by candle-light, and that it was considered a sacred duty to expose a lighted candle in the windows of every house as the corpse was carried through the streets. He speaks of the custom as a mark of respect to the dead, but possibly there was something more than this in it. In Ireland even to-day it is usual to leave lighted candles in the room where a corpse is laid out.

This belief in the power of bells over not only demons and evil spirits of every kind, but also over the elves and 'good people,' appears to have been held in all countries ever inhabited by fairies and hill folk. The Danish trolls are said to have been driven out of the country by the hanging of bells in the churches, the noise reminding them forcibly of the time when Thor used to fling his hammer after them. It is recorded in a bit of local doggrel from the pen of a dead and forgotten rhymester, that the fairies remained at Saddleworth, on the confines of Lancashire and Yorkshire, until'The steeple rose,And bells began to play;'

when the Queen wandered away to the wild district'Where Todmore's kingdom lay;'

and the less important plebeians of fairy land 'disperséd, went.' Mr. Henderson says that 'at Horbury, near Wakefield, and at Dewsbury, on Christmas Eve, is rung the "devil's knell," a hundred strokes, then a pause, then three strokes, three strokes, and three strokes again.'

In Iceland it is believed that at daybreak or upon the ringing of a bell the trolls flee.

10.

Fairy funerals, according to tradition, have been seen in other counties beside Lancashire, for an old Welsh writer alludes to such sights as having been witnessed in his day. Mr. Wirt Sikes, in his _British Goblins_, a recent and most valuable contribution to the folk lore and mythology of South Wales, says that the bell of Blaenporth, Cardiganshire, was noted for tolling thrice at midnight, unrung by human hands, to foretell death, and that when the 'Tolaeth before the burying,' the sound of an unseen funeral-procession passing by, is heard, the voices sing the 'Old Hundredth,' and the tramping of feet and the sobbing and groaning of mourners can be heard. In Normandy, says P. Le Fillastre, _Annuaire de la Manche_, 1832, the large white coffins, _les bières_, which the belated voyager sees along the roads, or placed on the churchyard fences, are unaccompanied by either bearers or mourners, and the cemetery bell is silent.

Readers of Professor Hunt's volumes of Cornish Drolls and Romances will remember the beautiful legend of the fisherman who, gazing by night through the window of a lonely church, saw a procession passing along the aisle, and witnessed the interment, near the sacramental table, of the fairy queen. The only point of resemblance, however, between the Southern and Northern traditions is to be found in the solemn tolling of the church-bell. The Cornish story is unique in one respect, inasmuch as, although we have plenty of legends in which the fairies evince a desire to peer into their future state, and even some in which their deaths are alluded to, it is extremely rare to find one in which the burial of a fairy is narrated; and this fact would seem to point to a defect in the 'Finn theory,' so plausibly advocated by Mr. Campbell; for, surely, if once upon a time 'the fairies were a real people, like the Lapps,' tradition would not be so silent, as it almost universally is, with reference to the outward and visible signs of their mortality.[C]

[C] Only since these notes were in type have I seen the excellent paper from the pen of Mr. Grant Allen (_Cornhill Magazine_, March 1881), on the Genesis of the Myth of the Fairies. See also the same charming writer's _Vignettes from Nature_, p. 206, and papers by B. Melle and F. A. Allen, in _Science Gossip_ for 1866, 'The Track of the Pigmies.'

11.

My friend, Mr. W. E. A. Axon, in his interesting _Black Knight of Ashton_, tells a story of a 'Race with the Devil,' the hero of which was one of a party of _pace-eggers_, who, waking up after a doze by a farm-house fire, beside which the party had been permitted to sleep on a wild night, and, feeling cold, had put on his Beelzebub dress, to the terror of another member of the company, who awoke afterwards, and seeing, as he supposed, the Devil seated airing himself by the fire, fled into the darkness and the storm, his equally terrified companions following him, and the no-less-frightened Beelzebub bringing up the rear.

The Mid and South Lancashire stories, as will at once be seen, do not resemble each other in any way, however; and I refer to Mr. Axon's legend for the sake of directing my readers' attention to a valuable note appended to it, in which Mr. Axon points out that there is a similar old Hindoo story of such a chase, which was translated from the Sanscrit into Chinese not later than the year 800.

It seems hardly probable that the Lancashire pace-egging story, so exquisitely narrated by my friend, could have had an Aryan origin, yet the resemblance is a striking and remarkable one.

12.

Many are the traditions of submerged bells told along the Lancashire coast. 'Here,' says the Rev. W. Thornber in the scarce _History of Blackpool_ (1844), 'or out at sea opposite this spot, once stood the cemetery of Kilgrimol, mentioned in the above-quoted chapter of the Priory of Lytham. Of this fact, tradition is not silent, and the rustic who dwells in the neighbourhood relates tales of fearful sights, and how many a benighted wanderer has been terrified with the sounds of bells pealing dismal chimes.' In Wales, too, the superstition is a common one. It is by no means improbable that there may be more in these faint whispers than would at first appear, and that underneath these dim traditions of churches swallowed by the sea there may rest a faint stratum of the old Scandinavian superstition that sweet singing and beautiful music could be heard by any who stood to listen on an Elf hill; for, although the idea of submerged cities may be found floating in the lore of all Celtic peoples, and in some places the submersion is a matter even of history,[D] in others, as at Kilgrimol, it is doubtful whether the sounds come from the sea or the earth. It is, therefore, more than likely that the traditions of submersion have received the addition of pealing bells from natural causes. There is an Indian superstition which in another way illustrates this theory. Manitobah Lake, in the Red River region, derives its name from a small island, upon which is heard, whenever the gales blow from the north, a sound resembling the pealing of distant church-bells, and which is caused by the waves beating on the shore at the foot of the cliffs and the rubbing of the fallen fragments against each other. This island the Ojibeways suppose to be the home of Manitobah, 'the speaking god,' and upon it they dare not land.

[D] _Vide_ Lyell's _Principles of Geology_, Chapter on _Encroachments of the Sea_, for many instances of submerged villages and churches along the English coast.

There is in Normandy a singular tradition of a submerged bell, dating back to the time of the English occupation, along with others of buried and hidden treasure. It is said that, as the English soldiers were abandoning the country, they destroyed the abbey of Corneville, and were taking away with them the principal bell, when the barge capsized. As they were trying to recover the prize, the French came upon them, and they were obliged to hurry away, leaving the bell behind. Since that time, whenever the bells of the churches in the district ring out their joyous peals upon solemn festival days, the submerged bell also can be heard joining in the carillon. (_Essai sur l'arrondissement de Pont-Audemer_.)

A story somewhat similar to this is told of a bell from St. David's, Pembrokeshire, carried off by Cromwellian troops whose vessel afterwards was wrecked in Ramsay Sound, from the moving waters of which the pealing can be heard when a storm is rising.

13.

For the sake of those who are not 'native and to the manner born,' Roger's story is not given in his vernacular, a mixture of the Mid-Lancashire and the Furness dialects, trying even to those who are acquainted with the expressive Doric of other parts of the County Palatine.

14.

Mr. Henderson, in his _Notes on the Folk Lore of the Northern Counties of England and the Borders_, states that Mr. Wilkie maintains that the _Digitalis purpurea_ was in high favour with the witches, who used to decorate their fingers with its largest bells; hence called Witches' Thimbles. Mr. Hartley Coleridge has more pleasing associations with this gay wild-flower. He writes of 'the faysThat sweetly nestle in the foxglove bells;'

and adds in a note, 'popular fancy has generally conceived a connection between the foxglove and the good people.' In Ireland, where it is called _lusmore_, or the great herb, and also Fairy Cup, the bending of its stalks is believed to denote the unseen presence of supernatural beings. The Shefro, or gregarious fairy, is represented as wearing the corona of the foxglove on his head, and no unbecoming head-dress either. In Wales, that the elves wear gloves of the bells of _Digitalis_ is a common fancy.

15.

This conventional circle seems to be universally common to such stories of summoning the Evil One. Even in China, as Mr. Dennys has stated, the ring is drawn round the summoner, and the incantation uttered, as in our own stories.

16.

In Lancashire, Old Nick (afterwards St. Nicholas, the patron saint of sailors) is considered the patron saint of the wind, just as in the Scandinavian mythology it is Odin, also termed Nick and Hold Neckar, who raises storms.

In Normandy, near Aigle, there is a superstition respecting a Mother _Nique_, doubtless, says Vaugeois, of Scandinavian origin.

17.

Instances of generous treatment of opponents on the part of the Evil One are by no means rare. Readers of Mr. Roby will remember that Satan gave a loophole of escape to Michael Waddington, the hero of 'Th' Dule upo' Dun' legend, by granting him an extra wish, although the poor wretch's time was up.

18.

The Cockerham schoolmaster appears to have lacked originality, for in the Scottish legend of 'Michael Scott' it is recorded that when the fairies crowded round his dwelling crying for work, he bade them twine ropes of sand to reach the moon, and tradition has it that traces of their unsuccessful attempts may yet be found. A more recent instance is told in a sketch of Dr. Linkbarrow, a Westmoreland wizard, who lived about a hundred years ago, quoted from the _Kendal Mercury_ by Mr. Sullivan, in his _Cumberland and Westmoreland, Ancient and Modern_. The Doctor, who was disturbed at church by a terrible storm, hurried home, and on the way met the devil, who asked for work. He immediately set him to make 'thumb symes' of river sand. Imitating the Israelites, perhaps not unconsciously--for Satan's knowledge of Scripture is proverbial-- the Evil One asked for straw, which was refused him. On his arrival at home, the Doctor found his servant prying into his black-letter book, which imprudence had caused the storm and Satan's pilgrimage.

Several similar stories, illustrating the danger of tampering with books of magic, are told in Normandy. In one of them it is recorded that the servant of a village curé, moved by curiosity, read a page or two of one of his master's volumes, when suddenly Satan appeared. The domestic fled, but the Evil One captured him, and was making away with him when the curé arrived and simply read a few other words from the book, upon which Satan dropped his prey. In another one Satan keeps his victim three years, but at length is obliged to let him go.

In the last story of this kind, however, which has come under my notice--a French one by the way--the incautious student has scarcely read a line of the open book when Satan appears and strangles him. The sorcerer, quietly returning home, sees devils perched on the house, and, surprised, beckons them to approach. One does so, and tells him the story, and he thereupon rushes to his study and finds the student stretched dead upon the floor. Afraid of being accused of murder, he orders the devil who had assassinated the scholar to pass into the body of his victim. The demon obeys, and goes to promenade in the street at the point most frequented by the students, but suddenly, upon another order, he quits the body, and the corpse falls in the midst of the terrified promenaders.

In Cornwall, instead of the devil, it is the ghost of Tregeagle, the wizard, that is doomed to make trusses of sand in Genvor Cove, and to bear them to the top of Escol's Cliff. Having once succeeded in carrying a truss, after having first brought water from a neighbouring stream and frozen the sand, he is now condemned to make the trusses without water.

19.

Another version of this story, which is still told in the lonely farm-houses of the district, gives the scholars the credit of having raised the devil during the absence of their master. Similar tasks were given to the infernal visitor by a sharp-witted lad, who feared lest his should be the soul the Evil One threatened to take back with him; and not many years ago a flag, said to have been broken by the outwitted Satan in his passage across the floor, used to be triumphantly exhibited to any daring and irreverent sceptic who expressed doubts as to the truthfulness of the narrative.

At Burnley Grammar School a black mark on a stone was at one time exhibited in proof of a state visit of the same kind, and a similar ignominious flight.

The Grammar School of Middleton, near Manchester, also can boast of the patronage of the Evil One; and Samuel Bamford has recorded that in his youth a hole in the school flags was shown as an impression of the Satanic hoof. The Middleton legend credits the lads with the unenviable honour of having called up the fiend and afterwards innocently wishing him to withdraw, which he sternly declined to do without having received his usual fee of a soul. As at Cockerham, he was requested to make a rope of sand; and he was rapidly completing the task, when, to the joy of the urchins, the schoolmaster came upon the scene, and quickly exorcised the visitor, who, in his disgusted and disordered flight, broke down nearly half of the building.

20.

Stories of headless beings may be found in the lore of most countries of Europe, and are of the same class as those of the men, women and horses 'beawt yeds,' common to the hilly districts of both North and South Lancashire. As a general rule, in South Lancashire, the head is not seen at all, whereas in the northern part of the county the spectre almost invariably carries it under the left arm, as is done by the wandering beings in similar Danish stories. A Scotch legend, alluded to by Sir Walter Scott, credits the ghost of a Duchess of Queensberry with an innovation, as the spectre is said to wheel its head in a barrow through the galleries of Drumlanrick Castle. In Glamorganshire there is a tradition of a headless woman, who appears every sixty years, and many are the terrible stories told of her dreadful visitations.

Although tales of headless horses are not rare in Lancashire, there does not appear to be any tradition of hearses, or other conveyances drawn by them, similar to the Northumberland legend of the midnight cavalcade along the subterraneous passage between Tarset and Dalby Castles, or to the stories told by the Irish peasants.

It is more than probable that many of the legends and stories of headless beings of both sexes had their origin in the old Saxon belief that if a person who was guilty of a crime for which he deserved to lose his head, died without having paid the penalty, he was condemned after death to travel over the earth with his head under his arm.

21.

Not very long ago it was commonly believed at Warrington, on the authority of many persons who declared they had seen the apparition, that a spectral white rabbit haunted Bank Quay, its appearance invariably foretelling the early death of a relative of the person whose misfortune it was to behold the animal.

'In Cornwall,' says Mr. Hunt, 'it is a very popular fancy that when a maiden who has loved not wisely but too well, dies forsaken and broken-hearted, she comes back in the shape of a white hare to haunt her deceiver. The phantom follows the false one everywhere, mostly invisible to all else. It sometimes saves him from danger, but invariably the white hare causes the death of the betrayer in the end.'

22.

Can this tradition be an offshoot of the legend of Ahasuerus, the Wandering Jew, the man who, standing at his door, refused the cup of water for which the Saviour, bowed down beneath the burden of the cross, begged, but who bade the Lord walk quicker, and was answered, 'I go, but thou shalt thirst and tarry till I come'? In one shape or another most European countries have the weird myth of this restless being. In none of the stories, however, have I found any reference to an animal accompanying the wanderer.

23.

The belief in the efficacy of fairy ointment appears to have been somewhat generally held in England. A Northumberland tradition tells of a midwife who was fetched to attend a lady, and who received a box of ointment with which to anoint the infant. By accident the woman touched one of her eyes with the mixture, and at once saw that she was in a fairy palace. She had the good sense, however, to conceal her astonishment, and reached her home in safety. Some time afterwards she saw the lady stealing bits of butter in the market-place, and thoughtlessly accosted her, when, after an inquiry similar to that of the Lancashire legend, the fairy breathed upon the offending eye and destroyed the sight. Other versions still current in Northumberland make the thief a fairy stealing corn. Similar stories are told in Devonshire and in both the Lowlands and Highlands of Scotland. In Scotland, however, the fairy spits into the woman's eye. The Irish fairy (Co. Wexford), a vindictive being, uses a switch.

In Cornwall a fairy bantling has to be put out to nurse, and has to be washed regularly in water and carried to its room by its invisible relatives. The nurse receives the marvellous sight after some of the liquid has splashed upon her eyes, and the usual result follows. She sees a thief in the market-place--that of St. Ives; and after he has muttered--'Water for elf, not water for self!You've lost your eye, your child, and yourself!'

she becomes blind. In another Cornish legend a green ointment, made with four-leaved clover, gathered at a certain time of the moon, confers the wondrous gift. In Lancashire the four-leaved clover does not require any preparation; the mere possession of it being supposed to render fairies visible.

The Scandinavian belief appears to have been that, although the hill folk could bestow the gift of this sight upon whom they chose, all children born on Sunday possessed the faculty. This superstition seems to survive in a slightly altered form in the Lancashire one that children born during twilight can see spirits and foretell deaths, the latter faculty, probably, having been substituted for the prophetic power of the chosen of the elves in the Northern mythology.

It is more than probable that these ointment stories came from the East. Who does not remember the charming history of the blind man, Baba Abdalla, whose sight was destroyed by a little miraculous ointment, and afterwards as wonderfully restored by a box on the ear?

24.

An old farm-labourer pointed out to me a place where the Evil One used to meet the witches, and gambol with them until cock-crow. It was at the junction of four cross-roads, between Stonyhurst and Ribchester; and as I stood there at 'th' edge o' dark,' when the wind was whispering through the fir woods on either hand, with that mysterious sound so like the gentle wash of waves upon a sandy shore, the spot seemed indeed a suitable one for such gatherings.

My informant, however, although very circumstantial in his account of what had transpired at the nocturnal assemblies, scouted the idea of anything of the sort taking place in these times, and remarked drily: 'Ther's too mich leet neaw-a-days, Mesthur, fur eawt o' that mak'. Wi' should hev' th' caanty police after um afooar they'd time to torn raand!'

25.

Until recently, there was an ancient British tumulus by the side of the highway from Darwen to Bolton, where the road passes through the domains of White Hall and Low Hill. This spot, long before the urns of bones were disinterred, was looked upon by the country people as being haunted by various boggarts, and Mr. Charles Hardwick says that children were in the habit of taking off their clogs and shoes, and walking past the heap barefooted when compelled to traverse the road after nightfall.[E]

[E] _Vide_ Footnote [C]

26.

Mag did not wander far, for her grave is shown in the churchyard at Woodplumpton, in which village her memory still is green. But few people venture to rest themselves upon the huge stone which marks the spot where her spirit was laid.

A strangely jumbled tradition tells how a priest managed to 'catch' her and 'lay her spirit.' In Cornwall and other counties a clergyman of the Establishment was considered qualified to 'lay' a ghost; but in Lancashire it was believed that only a Roman Catholic priest had the wondrous power. In Wales the magical number three is brought in, for three clergymen are necessary to exorcise a spirit. In Normandy, as a matter of course, only the priests have the power.

27.

Witchen or quicken, old English names of the rowan or mountain ash. Mr. Kelly (_Indo-European Tradition and Folklore_) accounts for the reputation of the 'wiggin' by connecting it with the Indian Palasa, the tree that, according to the Vedas, sprang from the feather which, together with a claw, fell from the falcon bringing the heavenly _soma_ to earth. The same writer also compares it with the Mimosa, and quotes a singular passage from Bishop Heber, to the effect that the natives of Upper India are in the habit of wearing sprigs of it in their turbans, and of suspending pieces of it over their beds, as security against wizards, spells, the Evil Eye, etc. Naturally enough the Bishop expresses his surprise at finding the superstitions, which in England and Scotland attach to the rowan, applied in India to a tree of similar form, and he asks, 'From what common centre are these common notions derived?' The Mimosa is popularly supposed to have sprung from the claw alluded to above.

On account of its reputed power against the 'feorin,' a rowan tree was almost invariably planted near the moorland or mountain side farm-house.'Rowan, ash, and red threadKeep the devils from their speed,'

says the old distich.

In some parts of Scotland ash sap still is given to infants as a preservative against fairies.

28.

It was firmly believed in Lancashire, says Mr. Harland, that a great gathering of witches assembled on this night at their general rendezvous in the Forest of Pendle--a ruined and desolate farm-house called the _Malkin Tower_ (Malkin being the name of a familiar demon in Middleton's old play of _The Witch_, derived from _maca_, an equal, a companion). This superstition led to another, that of _lighting_, _lating_, or _leeting_ the witches (from _leoht_, A.-S., light). It was believed that if a lighted candle were carried about the fells or hills from eleven to twelve o'clock at night, and it burned all the time steadily, it had so far triumphed over the evil power of the witches, who, as they passed to the Malkin Tower, would employ their utmost efforts to extinguish the light, that the person whom it represented might safely defy their malice during the season; but if by any accident the light went out, it was an omen of evil to the luckless wight for whom the experiment was made. It was also deemed inauspicious to cross the threshold of that person until after the return from leeting, and not then unless the candle had preserved its light. Mr. Milner describes the ceremony as having been recently performed.

29.

Mr. Sullivan quotes this quaint old carol at length in his _Cumberland and Westmoreland, Ancient and Modern_; and adds, 'This song is still sung at Penrith, having replaced one called "Joseph and Mary," in the early part of the century. Yet its antiquity is undoubted, and it has probably come here from Lancashire, where it is well known.'

As, however, it is by no means so widely known as Mr. Sullivan supposes, we may be pardoned if we reproduce it here. The second and remaining verses are as follows:--'I met three ships come sailing by,Come sailing by, etc.Who do you think was in one of them?In one of them? etc.The Virgin Mary and her Son,And her Son, etc.She combed His hair with an ivory comb,An ivory comb, etc.She washed His face in a silver bowl,A silver bowl, etc.She sent Him up to heaven to school,To heaven to school, etc.All the angels began to sing,Began to sing, etc.The bells of heaven began to ring,Began to ring, etc.'

30.

Mr. Samuel Bamford says that Middleton Parish Church was the scene of a procession similar to that described in the above legend, the observer being an avaricious old sexton who was anxious to know what fees he should receive in the following year. This worthy, on All Souls' night, stationed himself in the sacred building, and counted the spirits he saw enter and walk about, until he observed a double of himself. Of course, soon afterwards there was a vacancy for a gravedigger at Middleton, the sight having been too much for 'Old Johnny.'

A similar superstition reigns in various parts of England and in Wales, where, at Christmas-time, says Mr. Croker, quoting from a Welsh authority, the relatives of the deceased listen at the church door in the dark, 'when they sometimes fancy they hear the names called over in church of those who are destined shortly to join their lost relatives in the tomb.'

In Cornwall, strange to say, it is a young unmarried woman who, standing in the church porch at midnight on Midsummer's-eve, sees the strange gathering. 'This is so serious an affair,' says Professor Hunt, 'that it is not, I believe, often tried. I have, however, heard of young women who have made the experiment. But every one of the stories relate that they have seen shadows of themselves coming last in the procession; that pining away from that day forward, ere Midsummer has again come round they have been laid to rest in the village graveyard.'

Mr. Sikes says that it is a Hallow-Een custom in some parts of Wales to listen at the church door in the dark to hear shouted by a ghostly voice in the edifice the names of those who are shortly to be buried in the adjoining churchyard. In other parts, he says, 'the window serves the same purpose,' and, he adds, 'there are said to be still extant outside some village churches steps which were constructed in order to enable the superstitious peasantry to climb to the window to listen.' These steps in several places seemed to me to be merely old mounting blocks, but they may have been made use of for the less practical purpose in question.

31.

It is asserted that at the present day dogs cannot be induced to go near this quarry, and that even closely hunted animals will permit themselves to be captured rather than enter its recesses.

32.

Few superstitions have a wider circle of believers in Lancashire than that which attributes to dogs the power of foretelling death and disaster. There are few people, however well educated, who would be able to resist a foreboding of coming woe if they heard the howling of a strange dog under the window of a sick person's room; and, absurd as the dread so inspired may seem to the sceptic, there is more ground for it than can easily be explained away. It has frequently been urged that the animals are attracted by the lighted window, and that their howlings are nothing more than unpleasant appeals for admittance; and that often, by reason of the awe with which tradition has surrounded the noises, they terrify the invalid, and produce the end they are supposed to foretell. This plausible theory, however, does not account in any way for the similar visitations made in the daytime, when there is no artificial light to attract; or for the singular facts, that generally the dog is a stranger to the locality--that it does not loiter about, but makes its way direct to the particular house--that it will wait until a gate is opened, so that it may get near to the window--that it cannot be driven away before its mission has been performed--and that, in all cases, the howling is alike, invariably terminating in three peculiar yelping barks, which are no sooner uttered than the animal runs off, and is no more seen in the neighbourhood.

In Normandy the noise is considered an infallible presage of death.

Mr. Kelly says that this superstition obtains credence in France and Germany; and that in Westphalia, a dog howling along a road is considered a sure sign that a funeral soon will pass that way. In the Scandinavian mythology, Hel, Goddess of Death, is visible only to dogs.

The superstition has, at any rate, antiquity to recommend it, and it seems evident from Exodus xi. 5-7, that even in the days of the captivity of the Children of Israel in Egypt, the omen was firmly believed in.

I was seated one summer evening in the drawing-room of a house in one of the large London squares. The conversation was of the ordinary after-dinner nature, but enlivened by the remarks of more than one gifted guest. It was, however, suddenly interrupted in a very startling manner by the howling of a dog, which had placed itself in the roadway facing the house, regardless alike of the wheels of the numerous passing carriages and cabs, and of the whips of the drivers. The lady of the house, a north-country woman, said at once, as she rose from her seat at the open window, 'That means death. I shall hear of some sad trouble.' The dog would not be driven away by the angry coachmen and cabmen, but finished the howling with three peculiar yelps, and then trotted off rapidly; and there was much jesting during the rest of the evening about the strange occurrence. A few days afterwards, however, I was informed that on the evening of the dinner-party the brother of the hostess had died in North Lancashire.

33.

'Th' Gabriel Ratchets' strike terror into the heart of many a moorland dweller in Lancashire and Yorkshire still, presaging, as they are believed to do, death or sorrow to every one who is so unfortunate as to hear them. In the popular idea they are a pack of dogs yelping through the air. Our old literature has many references to the superstition. In more recent days, Wordsworth has introduced it in one of his sonnets:--

'And oftentimes will start--For overhead are sweeping GABRIEL'S HOUNDS.'

Mr. Philip Gilbert Hamerton, in a poem dated 1849, in his _Isles of Loch Awe and other Poems_, which he has kindly given me permission to quote here, says of them,--'Faintly sounds the airy note,And the deepest bay from the staghound's throat,Like the yelp of a cur, on the air doth float,And hardly heard is the wild halloo.'

and--'They fly on the blast of the forestThat whistles round the withered tree,But where they go we may not go,Nor see them as they fly.'

Mr. Hamerton, however, goes beyond the Lancashire peasant, at any rate so far as I have been able to ascertain, for I never met any one in the hill country or on the moorlands of the North who fancied that the throng included anything but _Ratchets_, _i.e._ dogs, for the poet goes on to sing--

'Hark! 'tis the goblin of the wood Rushing down the dark hill-side,With steeds that neigh and hounds that bay.'

Mr. Henderson has recorded that, about Leeds, the flight is supposed to be that of 'the souls of unbaptized children doomed to flit restlessly above their parents' abode.' In Germany, certainly the Wild Hunt or Furious Host is accompanied by unbaptized children, and it has been recorded that a woman, about the year 1800, died of grief upon learning that the Furious Host had passed over the village where her still-born child had died just before. Mr. Kelly (_Indo-European Tradition_) very ably and poetically resolves all the various superstitions of this Wild Hunt into figurative descriptions of natural phenomena, but Mr. Yarrell, the distinguished naturalist, reduces the cries of the Gabriel Hounds into the whistling of the Bean Goose, _Anser Segetum_, as the flocks are flying southward in the night, migrating from Scandinavia.

In Wales 'The Whistlers,' the cry of the golden-plover, is considered an omen of death, but it seems to be a quite distinct superstition from that of the _Cwn Annwn_, or Dogs of Hell, which latter is a Wild

Hunt.

I have heard the weird cry of the Gabriel Ratchets at night in several of the northern countries, and in the loneliness and gloom of early winter in the heart of the hills, or upon a wild bleak moorland, it was difficult to overcome a sudden feeling of dread when the yelps rang forth, even with Mr. Yarrell's scientific explanation fresh in my mind.

To sketch the ramifications of the superstition of the Wild Hunt, however, would require a volume, so numerous and various are they.

34.

In the old witch-mania records it is not unusual to find a cock sacrificed to the Evil One, and Satan's dislike of cock-crow has become proverbial. Brand has pointed out that the Christian poet Prudentius (fourth century) mentions that antipathy as a tradition of common belief. In an old German story Satan builds a house for a peasant who agrees to pay his soul for the work. A condition is made, however, that this house must be completed before cock-crow, and the wily peasant, just before the last tile is put on the roof, imitates the bird of morn, upon which all the cocks in the locality crow, and Satan, baffled, flees.

The Evil One's appearance in the form of a cat, a goat, a pig, an old woman, a black dog, a stylish gentleman, and the conventional shape, with hoof and horns, have been testified to, and Calmet (_Traité sur les apparitions des Esprits et sur les Vampires_, 1751) alludes to his taking the shape of a raven, but I have not met with any record of his appearance as a cock. In this case, however, that was insisted upon, although it was suggested that it might have been some other fowl.

www.ingramcontent.com/pod-product-compliance
Lightning Source LLC
Chambersburg PA
CBHW021325060726
47591CB00006B/1873